Alexa

RICHARD BOLITHO
- MIDSHIPMAN

ARROW BOOKS

Arrow Books Limited
3 Fitzroy Square, London W1

An imprint of the Hutchinson Publishing Group

London Melbourne Sydney Auckland
Wellington Johannesburg and agencies
throughout the world

First published by Hutchinson & Co (Publishers) Ltd 1975
Arrow edition 1977
© Bolitho Maritime Productions Ltd 1975

Made and printed in Great Britain
by The Anchor Press Ltd
Tiptree, Essex

ISBN 0 09 915200 2

For John and Betty Hamilton

Contents

I

A Ship of the Line

ALTHOUGH only noon, the clouds which scudded busily above Portsmouth harbour made it seem closer to evening. For several days a stiff easterly wind had turned the crowded anchorage into angry criss-crossing patterns of whitecaps, and an attendant drizzle gave each buffeted ship and the stout walls of the harbour defences a glistening, metallic sheen.

On Portsmouth Point itself, solid and uncompromising, stood the Blue Posts Inn. Like inns and hostelries in every busy seaport, it had been added to and altered over the years, but still retained an appearance of a sailor's haunt. In fact, it was used more by young midshipmen than any other seafarers who came and went with the tides, and because of this it held an atmosphere all of its own. Low-beamed, noisy and not particularly clean, it had seen more than one would-be admiral pass through its scarred doors.

On this particular day in mid-October 1772, Richard Bolitho sat wedged in a corner of one of the long rooms half listening to the babble of voices around him, the clatter of plates and tankards and the hiss of rain against the small windows. The air was heavy with mixed aromas. Food and ale, tobacco and tar, and each time the street doors opened to a chorus of curses and complaints the keener tang of salt from the waiting ships.

Bolitho stretched his legs and sighed. After the long and broken coach journey from his home in Falmouth, and a large portion of rabbit pie which was one of the Blue Posts' favourite dishes for the 'young gentlemen', he was feeling drowsy. He glanced curiously at the other midshipmen nearby. Some were very young. Children, no more than twelve years old at the most. He smiled, despite his normal reserve. When he had joined his first ship as midshipman he too had been twelve. Only by thinking back to that time could he appreciate how he had altered. How the Navy had changed him. He had been exactly like one of the boys along the table from him. Frightened, awed by the noise and outward hostility of a man-of-war, yet somehow determined not to show it, and always imagining that everyone else was entirely unimpressed by his surroundings.

And that had been four years ago. It was still difficult to accept. Four years in which he had matured and moulded to the ship around him. At first he had believed he would never be able to learn all that was asked and demanded of him. The bewildering complex of rigging and shrouds. The miles of cordage of every shape and length which made a ship move and obey. Sail drill and gun drill, up aloft on dizzily swaying yards in rain and sleet, or on days when it was so hot he had almost fainted and dropped to the deck far below. He had learned to understand the unwritten laws of the world between decks, the loyalties and rules which made everyday life possible in the overcrowded turbulent existence of a King's ship. He had not only survived, he had come through it better than he had thought possible. But not without some bruises and a few tears to mark his journey.

Now, on this dismal October day, he was joining his second ship, the seventy-four-gun *Gorgon*, which lay somewhere at anchor in the Solent.

He saw a small midshipman wolfing down a huge portion of boiled pork, and smiled grimly. He would live to regret it. It would be a long and lively pull in a boat through this wind.

He thought suddenly of his home in Cornwall, the great grey-stone house below Pendennis Castle where he and his brother and two sisters had grown up together. And where for that matter the Bolitho family had been living for generations. It had been different from what he had expected, from what he had dreamed about as he had endured storm and heat alike. For one thing, only his mother and sisters had been there to greet him. His father, who commanded a ship similar to the one he was joining, had been away in Indian waters. His older brother, Hugh, was senior midshipman in a frigate in the Mediterranean. The house had seemed quiet and very still after a ship of the line.

His new appointment had been delivered on his sixteenth birthday. To proceed with all despatch to His Britannic Majesty's Ship *Gorgon* at Spithead, which under the command of Captain Beves Conway was re-commissioning for duty in the King's name.

His mother had tried to hide her dismay. His sisters had laughed and cried as the fancy took them.

When he had made his way to board the Falmouth coach he had seen the farm workers nod to him as he had passed. But no show of surprise. For many, many years Bolithos had left the grey house to join one ship or another. Some of them had never returned.

And now it was all beginning again for Richard Bolitho. He had vowed that there were mistakes he would never repeat, some lessons he would remember above all else. A midshipman was neither fish nor fowl. He stood between the lieutenants and the true backbone of any vessel, the warrant officers. At one end of the ship, aloof and unreachable like some sort of god, was the captain. Above, around and beyond the overcrowded midshipmen's berth were the ship's company. Seamen and marines, volunteers and pressed men alike, packed together between decks, yet at all times separated by status and experience. Harsh discipline was the rule rather than the exception, danger and death from working the ship in all weathers were too common-place to mention.

When landsmen saw a King's ship working clear

of the shore, her yards alive with sailors and freshly set sails, when they heard the bang of gun-salutes, the lusty voices of those at the capstan joining in a well-tried shanty, they knew nothing of that other world within the deep hull. Which was probably just as well.

'Anyone sitting here?'

Bolitho came out of his thoughts and looked up. Another midshipman, fair-haired and blue-eyed, was smiling at him.

The newcomer added, 'Martyn Dancer. I'm joining the *Gorgon*. The landlord pointed you out to me.'

Bolitho introduced himself and moved along the bench.

'Not your first ship.'

Dancer smiled sadly. 'Almost. I was in the flag-ship until she went into dock. My experience amounts to three months and two days.' He saw Bolitho's expression. 'I started late. My father was unwilling to let me go to sea.' He shrugged. 'But I had my way in the end.'

Bolitho liked what he saw. Dancer had certainly begun his sea career late. He was about his own age, and had the quiet, cultured voice of a good family. A town family, he decided.

Dancer was saying, 'I have heard that we are sailing for West Africa. But then . . .'

Bolitho grinned. 'It is as good a rumour as any. I heard it too. It will be better than beating back and forth with the Channel Fleet.'

Dancer grimaced. 'The Seven Years War has been

over for nine years. I'd have thought the French would be at us again by now, if only to get their Canadian possessions back.'

Bolitho turned as two crippled seamen approached the landlord who was watching one of his girls ladling stew into pewter pots.

No real war for nine years. It was true enough. And yet there were still other conflicts around the world which never stopped. Uprisings and piracy, colonies fighting their new masters, they had claimed as many victims as any line of battle.

The landlord said harshly, 'Be off with you! I want no beggars here!'

One of the sailors, his right arm amputated almost to the shoulder, retorted angrily, 'I'm no bloody beggar! I was in the old *Marlborough*, seventy-four, with Rear-Admiral Rodney!'

There was complete silence in the long room, and Bolitho saw that several of the younger midshipmen were staring at the two cripples with something like horror.

The second man exclaimed anxiously, 'Leave it be, Ted! The devil will give us nothin'!'

Dancer said, 'Give them all they need.' He dropped his eyes, confused and angry. 'I will pay.'

Bolitho looked at him, sharing his concern. His shame.

'That was well said, Martyn.' He touched his sleeve impetuously. 'I am glad we are joining together.'

They both looked up as a shadow fell between them and one of the smoky lanterns.

The one-armed man was staring at them, his face very grim.

He said quietly, 'Thank you, young gentlemen.' He thrust out his hand. 'Good luck go with you. I reckon I'm seeing two captains.'

He moved away as one of the serving girls carried two steaming pots of food to a side table, adding for the room's benefit, 'Some of you take heed of this day. A lesson for you.'

The landlord thrust his large bulk towards the midshipmen as the buzz of conversation slowly returned.

'I'll take your damn money *now*!' He glared at Dancer. 'And after that . . .'

Bolitho said calmly, 'After *that*, landlord, you will bring two glasses of brandy for us.' He watched the man's mounting fury, gauging the moment as he would the fall of a nine-pound shot. 'I would mind your manners if I were you. My friend here is fortunately in good humour. But his father owns most of the land around this point.'

The landlord swallowed hard. 'But, God bless you, sir, I was only teasing! I'll bring the brandy at once. The best I have, and I trust you will allow me to pay for it.' He hurried away, his face suddenly worried.

Dancer said incredulously, 'But my father is a tea merchant in the City of London! I doubt if he has ever seen Portsmouth Point in his life!' He shook his head. 'I think I shall have to sharpen my wits if I am to keep pace with you, Richard!'

Bolitho smiled gravely. '*Dick*, if you don't mind.'

As they were sipping their brandy the street door was flung wide open. This time it did not close. Framed in the entrance was a lieutenant in a streaming tarpaulin coat, his cocked hat sodden from spray and rain.

He barked, 'All midshipmen for the *Gorgon* to muster at the sallyport at once. There is a party of men outside to take your chests to the boat.'

He strode to the fire and snatched a goblet of brandy from the landlord.

'It's blowing like hell outside.' He held his reddened hands above the blaze. 'God help us.'

As an afterthought he added, 'Who is the senior amongst you?'

Bolitho saw the anxious exchange of glances, the way that the snug contentment had given way to something like panic.

He said, 'I think I am, sir. Richard Bolitho.'

The lieutenant eyed him suspiciously. 'So be it. March 'em to the sallyport and report to the boat's cox'n. I will be along shortly.' He raised his voice. 'And when I get there, I want every mother's son of you ready to leave, see?'

The smallest midshipman said desperately, 'I think I'm going to be sick!'

Somebody laughed, but the lieutenant roared, 'You're going to be sick, *sir*! Say *sir* when you address an officer, damn you!'

The landlord's wife watched the untidy cluster of midshipmen hurrying towards the rain.

'Yew'm a bit hard on 'em, Mr Hope, sir.'

The lieutenant grinned. 'We all had to go through

it, m'dear. Anyway, the captain's difficult enough as it is, what with one thing and t'other. If I'm adrift with the new midshipmen then *I'll* be in for a broadside!'

Outside on the wet cobbles Bolitho watched some seamen loading the black chests into an assortment of barrows. Burly and tanned, they looked like experienced sailors, and he guessed that the captain was taking no chances by allowing less reliable members of his company ashore in case they deserted.

In weeks, even days, he would know these men and many more. He would not fall into the old traps as in his other ship. He knew now that trust was something you had to earn, not a gift which went with the uniform.

He nodded to the senior hand. 'We will move off directly.'

The man grinned at him. 'Not the first time for you then, sir?'

Bolitho fell in step beside Dancer. 'Or the last.'

At the sallyport they found the boat's coxswain sheltering behind the wall. Beyond it the Solent heaved and broke to endless ranks of cruising wave-crests, and against the leaden sky the few gulls looked like white spindrift.

The coxswain touched his hat. 'I suggest you get 'em all aboard, sir. There's quite a tide runnin' an' the first lieutenant wants the boat to do another trip afore the dog watches.' He dropped his voice. ' 'Is name is Mr Verling, sir. Be warned. 'E's a mite rough on some young gennlemen. Likes 'em to try their 'ands at everythin' 'e does.' He chuckled unfeelingly. 'Gawd, look at 'em. 'E'll 'ave 'em for breakfast.'

Bolitho snapped, 'And I *you*, if you don't stop gossiping.'

Dancer stared at him as the man hurried away.

Bolitho said, 'I've met his sort before, Martyn. The next minute he'd be asking permission to go off for a quick tot of rum.' He grinned. 'I think the lieutenant back there would be displeased, never mind the formidable Mr Verling.'

The officer in question appeared by the wall, his eyes somewhat glassy.

'Into the boat! Lively there!'

Dancer said quietly, 'I think maybe my father was right!'

Bolitho waited for the others to clamber down the slippery ladder towards the pitching longboat.

'I'm not sorry to go back to sea.' And he was surprised to find that he meant it.

The journey from the sallyport to the anchored two-decker took the best part of an hour. During the trip in the madly leaping longboat the midshipmen who managed to survive being violently sick had plenty of time to study their new home as she grew larger and taller through the relentless rain.

Bolitho had made it his business to learn something about his next appointment. Seventy-fours, as these sturdy two-deckers were nicknamed, made up the bulk of the fleet. In any big sea battle they were always predominant in the line where the fighting was hardest. And yet he knew from experience, and what he had heard old sailors say, that each one was as different from the other as salt from molasses.

While the oarsmen pulled the boat over each angry crest he kept his attention on the ship, seeing the towering masts and crossed yards, the shining black and buff hull with its lines of closed gunports, the scarlet ensign at her high stern and the jack at her bows making patches of colour against the background of grey sea and sky. The oarsmen were getting tired from their hard efforts, and it took the repeated stroke from the coxswain and several threats from the red-faced lieutenant to keep them working in unison.

Around and under the long bowsprit and jib-boom, beneath which the brightly gilded figurehead seemed to stare down at the silent midshipmen with something like hatred. It was a splendid if frightening example of a wood-carver's art. The *Gorgon*'s figurehead was a mass of writhing serpents, the face below set in a fierce glare, the eyes very large and edged with red paint to give an added effect of menace.

And then, panting and scrabbling, they were being pushed, hauled and bundled unceremoniously up the ship's side, so that when they arrived on the broad quarterdeck it seemed almost sheltered and calm by comparison.

Bolitho said, 'She looks smart enough, Martyn.'

He ran his eyes quickly along the neat lines of the quarterdeck nine-pounders, their black barrels gleaming in the rain, the trucks freshly painted, every piece of tackle neat and carefully stowed.

Seamen were working aloft on the yards and along the gangways on either beam which joined quarterdeck to forecastle. Beneath the gangways, at the same regular intervals, were the upper deck batteries of eighteen-pounders, while on the deck below them were the ship's main armament of powerful thirty-two pounders. When required, *Gorgon* could and would speak with loud authority.

The lieutenant shouted, 'Over here!'

The midshipmen hurried to obey, some fearful and already lost. Others wary and careful to watch what was required of them.

'In a moment you will go to your quarters.' The lieutenant had to raise his voice above the hiss of rain, the persistent din of wind through rigging and furled sails. 'I just want to tell you that you are now appointed to one of the finest ships in His Majesty's Navy, one with high standards and no tolerance of laggards. There are twelve midshipmen all told aboard *Gorgon*, including yourselves, so the mothers' boys had best work doubly hard to avoid trouble. You will be given postings to gundecks and other parts of ship until you are able to work with the people without making a poor example to them.'

Bolitho turned as some men hurried past under the control of a tough-looking boatswain's mate. Fresh from the land by the cut of them, he thought. Taken from debtors' prisons and from the Assize Courts where but for the need of men for the fleet they would be held until transportation to the American colonies. The Navy's appetite for men was never satisfied, and with the country at peace it was even harder to supply its needs. As he watched the hurrying party of men Bolitho thought it hardly made sense of what the lieutenant had just said. Not only the midshipmen were new and untrained. Many of the ship's company were little better.

As he slitted his eyes against the rain he found time to marvel at the way a ship like this could swallow such a force of human beings. *Gorgon*, he knew, contained a company of some six hundred officers, seamen and marines in her fat, seventeen-hundred-ton hull, and yet to look along her upper deck it was hard to see more than thirty or so at any one time.

'*You!*'

Bolitho turned as the lieutenant's voice cut into his thoughts.

'I hope I am not boring you?'

Bolitho replied, 'I am sorry, sir.'

'I will be watching you.'

The lieutenant stiffened as another officer approached from the poop.

Bolitho guessed the newcomer to be the first lieutenant. Mr Verling was tall and thin, with an expression so dour that he could have been a judge about to pass sentence of death rather than offering welcome to some new officers. He had a protruding, beaked nose which thrust from beneath his cocked hat as if to seek out some new crime in his ship, and his eyes, as they wandered along the swaying line of midshipmen, were devoid of pity or warmth.

He said, 'I am the senior in this ship.' Even his tone was clipped, with all the compassion honed out of it. 'Whilst on board you will attend to your various duties at all times. You will become so involved with your training and preparation for examination as lieutenants that you will eventually put it before all else, and any sort of leisure will be seen even by you as both selfish and pointless.' He nodded to the other officer. 'Mr Hope is the fifth lieutenant and will be keeping an eye on you until you are settled in your allocated watches. Mr Turnbull, the master, will of course expect a high standard in navigational studies and the general working of the ship at sea.'

His gimlet eyes fastened on the smallest figure at the end of the line, the one who had been violently sick in the longboat, and who looked as if he was about to repeat it.

'And what is *your* name?'

'Eden, s-sir.'

'*Age?*' The word was like a knife cut.

'T-twelve, s-sir.'

Hope said, 'He has a stutter, sir.' Even his earlier belligerence had faded in the presence of his superior.

'Has he indeed. I am certain the boatswain will take care of that before he reaches thirteen years, *if* he lasts that long!'

Verling seemed to tire of the encounter. 'Dismiss them, Mr Hope. We will weigh tomorrow if the wind stays with us. There is much to do.' He strode away without another glance.

Hope said wearily, 'Mr Grenfell will take you below.'

Grenfell, it turned out, was the senior midshipman.

A thickset, unsmiling young man of about seventeen, he relaxed as soon as Hope had disappeared.

He said, 'Follow me. Mr Hope is a fair man, but he is worried about his promotion.'

Bolitho smiled. In a ship of the line promotion was always difficult, especially without a war to thin the ranks. As fifth lieutenant Hope had only one officer junior to himself in the wardroom, and unless the lieutenants above him were promoted, sent into other ships or killed he was hard put to find advancement.

Dancer whispered, 'In the flagship we had a sixth lieutenant who was so desperate that he learned to play the flute merely because the admiral's wife liked it!'

They fell silent as they followed the senior midshipman down the first companion ladder to the deck below, and the deck below that. The deeper they went into the hull the more confined it seemed to become. They were surrounded by shadowy figures, faceless and unreal in the half-darkness, their heads bowed beneath deck beams and the carefully slung equipment for each tethered cannon. The smells too seemed to rise to meet them. Salt beef and tar, bilge and packed humanity, while all around them the massive hull creaked and groaned like a live thing, the deckhead lanterns spiralling and throwing shapes across the great timbers and seamen alike, as in part of a vast painting.

The midshipmen's berth was on the orlop deck. Beneath the lower gundeck, and indeed lower than the waterline itself, it had no light other than from the hatches and the swaying lanterns.

Grenfell said offhandedly, 'This is it. We share it with the senior master's mates.' He grimaced towards a white-painted screen. 'Although *they* choose to stay aloof from us.'

Bolitho looked at his companions. Without difficulty he could imagine what they were feeling. He could recall how he had endured the first hours, how he would have given anything for a friendly word when it was most needed.

He said, 'It looks fine. Better than my last ship.'

The boy called Eden asked, *'Really?'*

Grenfell smiled. 'It's what you make it.' He swung round as a diminutive figure scrambled past the screen door. 'This is your servant. His name is Starr, but he doesn't say much. Just tell him what you need and I'll arrange it with the purser.'

Starr was even younger than Eden. Probably about ten, and small for his age. He had the pinched features of a child from the slums, and his arms were so thin they were like sticks.

Bolitho asked quietly, 'Where are you from?'

The boy eyed him warily. 'Newcastle, sir. Me dad was a miner there. He was killed in a fall.' His voice was toneless, as if he was speaking of another world.

'I'll damn well kill *you* if you treat my shirts like this one!'

Bolitho turned as another midshipman, flushed from the wind and rain, strode beneath the low beams. With Grenfell he was obviously one of the ship's three midshipmen remaining from the last commission, and like Grenfell too, still awaiting the chance to sit an examination for lieutenant.

He was in ill humour, and had the sullen good looks of one bred to authority.

Grenfell said, 'Easy, Samuel. The new boys are with us.'

The other one seemed to realize he was surrounded with awkward looking newcomers and snapped, 'I'm Samuel Marrack. Signals midshipman and captain's messenger.'

Dancer said, 'It sounds important.'

Marrack stared at him. 'It is. And when you appear before our illustrious captain it is best to do it in a clean shirt!' He lashed out at the small servant with his hat and added, 'So remember that in future, you hound!'

He threw himself on to a chest. 'Get me some wine. I'm as dry as dust.'

Bolitho sat down beside Dancer and watched the others opening and shutting their chests like blind men. He had hoped to be appointed to a frigate like his brother. Free of the fleet's heavy authority, able to cover great distances in a third of the time it would take the ponderous *Gorgon*, and with all the possibilities of adventure he had so often dreamed of.

But *Gorgon* was his new home, and he would have to make the best of her for as long as the Navy dictated. A ship of the line.

2

Outward Bound

'All hands! All hands aloft to reef tops'ls!'

Like the insistent voice in a nightmare the order was piped and repeated along the *Gorgon*'s decks until the ship quivered to the thud of feet as the watch below dashed to their stations to be mustered.

Bolitho shook Dancer roughly by the shoulder until he almost fell from his hammock.

'Come on, Martyn! We're shortening sail again!'

He waited as Dancer dragged on his shoes and coat and then together they ran for the nearest ladder. Three, no nearly four days it had gone on like this. From the moment the seventy-four had weighed anchor and started her passage down-channel towards the Atlantic it had been an endless turmoil of re-setting sails, of dragging weary bodies up the shrouds to the vibrating yards, and all the while harried and driven by the first lieutenant's voice from the quarterdeck. Even that had been part of the nightmare, for to make his orders heard above the roar of sea and wind Verling had had to use his speaking trumpet, making his sharp voice a ceaseless goad for the gasping midshipmen.

For the new hands it was always worse, of course. A midshipman had very little status in a King's ship. The common seaman had none at all.

Bolitho knew that to allow any break in discipline at a moment like changing a ship's tack in a heavy wind could be disastrous, but he was sickened to see unnecessary violence used on a man who was perhaps too terrified by working high above the deck to understand what was required of him.

It was no different from the last time. Not yet dawn, but there was a paler hint of grey showing itself in the low clouds, and precious little else to light a way to the shrouds. Lieutenants fretted impatiently as petty officers and master's mates checked their lists of names at the foot of each mast. The marines clumped aft to the mizzen braces, their boots skidding on wet planking, and by the quarterdeck rail the first lieutenant bobbed and pointed, waving his speaking trumpet to emphasize some point or other.

Bolitho peered aft to the big double wheel. Four helmsmen were clinging to the spokes so that he guessed there was still a big swell running to test the thrust of sails and rudder. Beside them he could see old Turnbull, the sailing master, shapeless in his heavy coat, his fists like red crabs as he gestured to his quartermaster.

Quite alone by the weather nettings was the captain. He was wrapped in a long boatcloak, but his hair blew in the wind while he peered up at the

reefed topsails, which with the jib were the only
canvas they were able to carry in such a gale.

Bolitho had got no nearer than this to his captain
since he had come aboard. In the distance he looked
very cool and dignified, apparently untouched by the
confusion of hurrying seamen and bawling petty
officers.

Dancer gritted his teeth. 'God, I'm near frozen.'

Lieutenant Hope, who was responsible for the
foremast, yelled, 'Take 'em aloft, Mr Bolitho! And
I want the time cut by minutes before I'm satisfied!'

A whistle shrilled and it all started again. The
nimble-footed topmen racing each other up the ratlines while the new hands and less confident followed
behind them pursued by threats and not a few blows
from the petty officers' rattans to hurry them
along.

And above it all Verling's voice, distorted and
inhuman through his trumpet, controlling and
steering everyone.

'Another pull on the weather forebrace! Mr
Tregorren, there's a man in your division who needs
starting, damn your eyes, sir! Two more hands aft to
the mizzen braces!' He never stopped.

Up those rough, shaking ratlines and around the
futtock shrouds, hanging out and down above the
hull and creaming sea below, clinging with fingers
and toes to keep from falling. Then breathless on to
the foretop, with men already scrambling further
still to the topsail yard, swarming out on either beam
like monkeys, clawing and fisting the thick, half-

frozen canvas to control it, to take in another reef while each billowing section did its best to knock the men from their perches and hurl them aside. Curses and sobs, men swearing terrible oaths as fingernails were torn out by the rough heavy-weather canvas; or they fought off their more frightened companions who clung to them for support.

Bolitho gripped a backstay and watched the scene on the other masts. It was almost done, and the ship was answering to the lesser thrust in her sails. Far below, foreshortened like dwarfs, he saw the quarter-deck officers and the afterguard who were securing their halliards and braces. Still by the weather side, the captain was watching the yards. Was he worried? Bolitho wondered. He certainly did not look it.

'*Secure, Mr Hope!*' Verling could not resist adding, 'You seem to have some cripples in your division! I suggest extra sail drill in the forenoon!'

Bolitho and Dancer slid to the deck on a backstay to find Mr Hope fuming again.

'God damn it, I shall swing for that one!' Hope recovered himself and added, 'And for you too, if you don't drive the people harder!'

As Hope strode aft Bolitho said, 'His bark is worse than his bite. Come on, Martyn, let us see what young Starr has saved us for breakfast. There is no point in climbing into a hammock now. They will call the hands directly.'

They found a reedy, severe-looking man in a plain blue coat waiting in the midshipmen's berth when they hurried breathlessly into its damp security. Bolitho already knew his name was Henry Scroggs,

the captain's clerk, who messed with their neigh-
bours, the master's mates.

Scroggs snapped, 'Bolitho, is it not?' He did not
wait for an answer. 'Report to the captain. Mr
Marrack has injured his arm and Mr Grenfell has
the morning watch.' He waited, his face impassive.
'Well, sir, jump to it, if you wish to draw breath
again!'

Bolitho stared at him, recalling what Marrack had
said about clean shirts, conscious of his own dishevelled appearance.

Dancer offered, 'Here, let me help you get
dressed.'

The clerk snapped, 'No time. Next to Grenfell and
Marrack, you are senior, Bolitho. The captain is very
definite about such matters.' He swayed as the ship
tilted steeply and sent the sea boiling loudly over the
upper deck. 'I suggest you make a move!'

Bolitho reached for his hat and said ruefully, 'Very
well.' Then ducking beneath the low deckbeams he
made his way aft.

Bolitho stood breathing hard outside a white-
painted screen door beneath the poop. After the
crowded quarters between decks, the shadowy figures
of the seamen returning from the work on the yards, it
seemed very quiet. Beside the door, standing rigidly
in a pool of light from a deckhead lantern, a marine
sentry regarded him coldly before calling, 'Signal
midshipman, *sir*!' He further emphasized the introduction by banging the butt of his musket smartly on
the deck.

The door opened, and Bolitho saw the captain's servant beckoning him urgently, holding the door open just sufficiently to allow him to enter. Like a footman in a fine house who is not sure of an unwelcome visitor.

'If you would wait 'ere,' pause, 'sir.'

Bolitho waited. It was a fine lobby which opened on to the captain's dining room and which ran the whole breadth of the hull. Glass tinkled quietly in a large mahogany cabinet, while above the long polished table a circular tray of bottles and decanters swung evenly to the ship's motion. The deck was covered in canvas, well-painted in black and white squares, and the nine-pounder cannon on either side of the cabin were discreetly hidden under chintz covers.

The door in a further screen opened and the servant said, 'This way, sir.' He was watching Bolitho with something like despair.

The great cabin. Bolitho stood just inside the door, his cocked hat wedged beneath one arm as he stared at the broad expanse of his captain's domain.

The cabin was splendid, and made further so by the huge stern windows which were so streaked with salt and dappled spray that in the grey dawn light they looked like those of a cathedral.

Captain Beves Conway was sitting at a large desk, leafing slowly through a sheaf of papers. A mug of something hot was steaming by his elbow, and as the lantern above the desk swung this way and that Bolitho saw that he was already dressed in a clean shirt and breeches, and his blue coat with its broad white lapels was laid carefully on a bench seat, his hat and boatcloak nearby. There was nothing about the man's face or appearance to suggest he had just returned from the deck and the bitter wind.

He looked up and studied Bolitho without expression.

The captain said, 'Name?'

'Bolitho, sir.' His voice sounded different in the broad cabin.

'Yes.'

The captain half turned as his clerk entered the cabin by another small door. In the lamplight and the angled glow from the stern windows Beves Conway had an alert, intelligent profile, but his eyes were hard and gave nothing away.

He was speaking curtly to Scroggs, his tone clipped, matter of fact, about things which Bolitho could only guess at.

He glanced to one side and saw himself for the first time in a long, gilt-framed mirror. No wonder the cabin servant had looked worried.

Richard Bolitho was tall for his years, tall and slim, with hair so black that it made his tanned features seem pale. In his seagoing coat, one which he had bought eighteen months earlier and had all but grown out of, he looked more like a vagrant than a King's officer.

He realized with a start that the captain was speaking to him.

'Well, Mr Midshipman, er, Bolitho, due to unforeseen circumstances it seems I must rely on your skills to assist my clerk until Mr Marrack is recovered from his, er, injury.' He regarded him calmly. 'What duties have you in my command?'

'Lower gundeck, sir, and with Mr Hope's division for sail drill.'

'Neither of those require that you should look like a dandy, Mr, er, Bolitho, but in my ship I need all my officers to set a perfect example, no matter what duty they are performing. As a junior officer you will be ready for anything. In this command you *lead*, you set an example, and wherever this ship takes you, you will not only represent the Navy, *you will be the Navy*!'

'I understand, sir.' Bolitho tried again. 'We had been aloft to shorten sail, sir, and . . .'

'Yes.' The captain gave what might have been a wry smile. 'I gave that order. I had been on deck for several hours before I decided it was really necessary.' He pulled a slim gold watch from his breeches. 'Return to your berth on the orlop and put yourself to rights. I want you aft again in ten minutes.' He closed the watch with a snap. 'Precisely.'

They were the shortest ten minutes in Bolitho's memory. Helped by Starr and Midshipman Dancer, and hindered by the luckless Eden, who chose the moment to be sick again, he eventually found his way aft to confront the same sentry by the door, but to discover the great cabin already busy with visitors. Lieutenants with questions or reports on storm damage. The master, who, from what Bolitho could gather, was either for or against the possible promotion of one of his mates. Major Dewar of the ship's marines, his jowls as scarlet as his uniform, even the purser, Mr Poland, a veritable weasel of a man, appeared to be calling on the captain. And it was only dawn.

The clerk led Bolitho unceremoniously to a small desk by the streaming quarter windows. Outside, through the thick glass, he saw the dull grey sea, the long streaks of breaking foam on every crest. A cluster of gulls dipped and wheeled around the *Gorgon's* high counter, obviously expecting something to be flung overboard by the cook. Bolitho felt his stomach contract. They would be unlucky, he thought. Between them, the cook and the miserly purser left few scraps for gulls.

He heard the captain discussing fresh water with Laidlaw, the surgeon, and something about scouring the empty casks to make them purer for a long voyage.

The surgeon was a tired-looking man with deep, hooded eyes and a permanent stoop. Too long in small ships, or too long bent over his luckless victims, Bolitho could only guess.

He was saying, 'It's a bad bit of coast there, sir.'

The captain replied tersely, 'I know that, damn it. I did not choose to take this ship and all her people to the west coast of Africa just to test your ability at curing ills!'

The clerk leaned over the little desk. He had a dank smell, like unwashed bedding.

He said dourly, 'You can begin by copying these orders for the captain. Five of each. Nice and clear, with a firm hand, or you'll be in trouble.'

Bolitho waited for Scroggs to shuffle away and then

cocked his ear towards the little group around the captain. While he had been struggling into one his clean shirts and a fresh neckcloth, he had discovered that his first awe at meeting the captain had begun to shift to resentment. Conway had dismissed his reason for being improperly dressed as unimportant, even trivial. In its place he had presented his own image, that of the captain always on call, tireless, and never without a solution for anything.

But now, as he listened to Conway's calm, unhurried voice, the mention of some four thousand miles to be sailed, the most profitable courses to be used, food, fresh water, and above all the training and efficiency of the company, he could only marvel.

In this cabin, which for a few moments he had regarded as the height of luxury, the captain fought his own private battles. He could share his anxieties with nobody, could divide his responsibility not at all. Bolitho shivered. The great cabin could become a prison for any man who lost his way in doubt.

He recalled his own childhood when he had visited his father's ship on those rare and privileged occasions when she had anchored at Falmouth. How different it had been. His father's officers smiling and friendly, some almost subservient in his presence. Rather different from his later introduction as a midshipman, when lieutenants had appeared bad tempered and intolerant.

Scroggs was at his side again.

'Take this message to the boatswain and come back immediately.' He thrust a folded piece of paper into his hand.

Bolitho picked up his hat and hurried past the big desk. He was almost through the screen door when the captain's voice halted him in his tracks.

'*What* did you say your name was?'

'Bolitho, sir.'

'Very well. Be off with you, and mark what I said.' Conway looked down at his papers and waited for the door to close.

When he glanced up again at the surgeon he said shortly, 'No better way to inform the people of what we are about than to let a new midshipman overhear.'

The surgeon regarded him gravely. 'I think I know that boy's family, sir. His grandfather was with Wolfe at Quebec.'

'Really.' Conway was already studying the next paper.

The surgeon added softly, 'He was a rear-admiral, sir.'

But Conway was elsewhere in his thoughts, his features set in a small frown.

The surgeon sighed. Captains were quite unreachable.

3

The City of Athens

SOUTH-WEST and then south, day in day out, with barely a pause from backbreaking work. While the *Gorgon* thrust her heavy bulk clear of the English Channel and headed down towards the notorious Bay of Biscay, Bolitho and his new companions drew closer together, as if to use their combined strength against the ship and the sea.

He had heard Turnbull, the master, say that the weather was as bad as he could recall for the time of year, and for someone who had seen some thirty winters in the Navy it was a statement to be taken seriously. Especially now that Bolitho had lost his temporary work in the great cabin. When Marrack had returned to duty after injuring his arm in the first storm, Bolitho had joined Dancer at the foremast whenever the call to make or shorten sail had been piped.

If he found a moment to consider his progress in his new ship, which was not often, Bolitho thought more of his physical than his mental state. He was always hungry, and every muscle and bone seemed to ache from constant climbs aloft or the other demands of gun drill on the lower batteries of thirty-two-pounders. When the sea and wind moderated, and *Gorgon* headed south under almost a full set of canvas, the ship's company went to quarters to learn, exercise and sweat blood over the heavy and cumbersome tiers of guns. On the lower deck it was made doubly difficult by the lieutenant in charge.

Grenfell, the senior midshipman, had already warned Bolitho about him, and as long days ran into longer weeks, while the ship pushed her beakhead between the Madeiran Islands and the coast of Morocco, all invisible even to the masthead lookouts, the name of Mr Piers Tregorren, the fourth lieutenant and the master of *Gorgon*'s twenty-eight heaviest cannon, took on new importance.

The fourth lieutenant was a massive figure, with the swarthy skin and lank hair more suitable to Spaniard or gypsy than a sea officer. The beams of the shadowy gundeck were so low that Tregorren had to duck and rise between them as he strode forward or aft to supervise the practice loading and running-out of each weapon. Big, belligerent and impatient, he was a hard man to serve.

Even Dancer, who was usually so busy keeping out of trouble that he saved his strength for eating and sleeping, had noticed that Tregorren seemed to have taken a dislike to Bolitho. It was strange, Bolitho thought, for Tregorren was a fellow Cornishman, and usually that was one bond which survived even the cuts and bruises of discipline.

Because of this animosity Bolitho had received three lots of extra duty, and on another occasion had been sent to the foremast crosstrees in a savage wind until ordered by the officer of the watch to descend. Harsh, unfair, it certainly was, but the punishment brought other sides of shiplife into the open. Young Eden produced a pot of honey which his mother had given him, and which he had been saving for some suitable occasion. Tom Jehan, the gunner, a really unsympathetic warrant officer, who messed beyond the screen and rarely deigned to speak with lowly midshipmen, brought a large mug of brandy from his private stock to restore some life to Bolitho's frozen body.

The endless, unrelenting training on sail and gun took other tolls, too.

Before they had even passed Gibraltar two men were lost overboard, and another died after falling from the mainyard and breaking his back on an eighteen-pounder. He was buried at a brief, but to the new men, moving ceremony, his corpse sewn in a hammock and dropped overboard weighted with roundshot, while the *Gorgon* titled steeply to a brisk north-easterly.

Further strains showed themselves like cracks in metal. Arguments broke out amongst the seamen, some trivial, some less so. A man turned on a boatswain's mate who had ordered him aloft for the third time in a watch to splice some worn rigging and was consequently taken aft to be awarded punishment.

Bolitho had seen his first flogging at the age of twelve and a half. He had never grown used to it, but he knew what to expect. The newer and younger midshipmen did not.

First came the pipe, 'All hands lay aft to witness punishment!' Next the rigging of a grating on one of the gangways, while the marines trooped athwartships across the poop, their scarlet coats and white crossbelts very clear against the dull, overcast sky. The ship's company seemed to swell out of every hatchway and hiding place, until the decks, shrouds and even the boat tier were crammed with silently watching figures.

And then the little procession wended its way to the rigged grating. Hoggett, the boatswain, and his two mates, Beedle, the unsmiling master-at-arms, Bunn, the ship's corporal, with the prisoner and Laidlaw, the surgeon, bringing up the rear. On the quarterdeck, its pale planking dappled with droplets of spume and spray, the officers and warrant officers took their places in order of seniority and importance. By the lee side the midshipmen, all twelve of them, made two short ranks on their own.

The prisoner was stripped and then seized up on the grating, his muscled back pale against the scrubbed wood, his face hidden as he listened to the captain's austere voice as he read the relevant Articles of War before finishing with, 'Two dozen, Mr Hoggett.'

And so, between the staccato roll of a solitary marine drummer boy, who kept his eyes fixed on the mainyard above his head throughout the flogging, the punishment was carried out. The boatswain's mate who actually used the cat-o'-nine-tails was not a brutal man by nature. But he was powerfully built and had an arm like the branch of an oak. Also, he was well aware that to show leniency would probably invite his changing places with the luckless offender. After eight strokes the seaman's back was a mass of blood. After a dozen it was barely recognizable as human. And so it went on. The roll of the drum and the immediate crack of the lash across the naked back.

The youngest midshipman, Eden, fainted, and the second youngest, a pale-faced youth called Knibb, burst into tears, while the rest and not a few of the watching seamen were stiff-faced with horror.

After what seemed like an age Hoggett called hoarsely, 'Two dozen, sir!'

Bolitho made himself breathe in and out very slowly as he watched the man being cut down from the grating. His back was torn as if mauled by some beast, the skin quite black from the force and weight of the lash. At no time had he cried out, and for a moment Bolitho imagined he had died under punishment. But the surgeon looked up at the quarterdeck as he prised the leather strap from between the man's teeth and reported, 'He's fainted, sir.' Then he beckoned his assistants to carry the man below to the sick-bay. The blood was swabbed from the deck, the grating removed, and as the drummer and two other young marines with fifes struck up a lively jig the company slowly returned to normal life once again.

Bolitho glanced quickly at the captain. He was expressionless, his fingers tapping a little tattoo on his sword-hilt as if in time with the jig.

Dancer exclaimed fiercely, 'What a foul way to treat a man!'

The old sailing master overheard him and rumbled, 'Wait till you've seen a flogging round th' fleet, m'lad, then you will have something to puke on!'

And yet, when the hands went for their mid-meal of salt beef and iron-hard biscuits, washed down with a pint of coarse red wine, Bolitho heard no word of complaint or anger from anyone. It seemed that as in his last ship the rule of the lower deck was that if you got caught you were punished. The fault was being found out.

This acceptance was even showing itself in the midshipmen's berth. The first anxiety and awe at not knowing what to do, and when to do it, had given way to a new unity, a toughness which had touched even Eden.

Food and comfort were paramount, and the uncertainty of the voyage, what they were being ordered to do, took on less importance.

The small compartment which nestled against the ship's curved side had become their home, the space between the white screen door and their heavy chests an area where they ate their crude meals, shared their confidences and fears and learned from one another with each succeeding day.

Apart from the sighting of a few murky islands and two distant ships, *Gorgon* seemed to have the ocean to herself. Daily the midshipmen gathered aft for instruction in navigation under Turnbull's watchful eye. The sun and the stars took on new meaning to some of them, while to the older ones the reality of promotion to lieutenant seemed not so distant and improbable.

After a particularly bad gun drill with the thirty-two-pounders Dancer said angrily, 'That man Tregorren has the devil in him!'

Little Eden surprised all of them by saying, 'He has the g-gout, if that is the d-devil, Martyn.'

They all stared at him as he added in his thin, piping voice, 'My f-father is an apothecary in B-Bristol. He is often c-called to t-treat such cases.' He nodded firmly. 'Mr Tregorren t-takes too much b-brandy for his own g-good.'

With this new knowledge at their disposal they were able to watch the fourth lieutenant's behaviour with more interest. Tregorren would lurch beneath the low deck beams, his shadow crossing the gun-ports like a massive spectre, while at each great cannon the crew would wait for the order to load and run out, to train or elevate as the lieutenant ordered.

Each gun weighed three tons and had a crew of fifteen hands to control it and its opposite number on the other side of the deck. Every man had to know exactly what to do, and to keep doing it no matter what. As Tregorren had shouted on many occasions, 'I'll make you bleed a bit, but it's nothing to what an enemy will do, so *move yourselves!*'

Bolitho was sitting at the slung table in the midshipmen's berth, a candle flickering in an old oyster shell to add some light to that which filtered from a nearby companionway, and writing a letter to his mother. He had no idea when, if ever, she would read it, but it gave him comfort to retain a link with his home.

From what he had gathered from his privileged position of aiding Turnbull with the navigation lessons, and his daily scrutiny of the master's charts, he knew that the first part of their passage was almost over. Four thousand miles, the captain had said, and as he had studied the wavering lines of the charts, the daily positions fixed by shooting the sun and the usual calculations on speed and course, he knew all the old excitement of an approaching landfall. Six weeks since weighing anchor at Spithead. Changing tack and constantly reducing or making sail. The ship's track wavered over the charts like an injured beetle. A speedy frigate would have covered the distance and been on her way back to England long since, he thought bitterly.

He paused, his pen in mid-air, as he heard muffled shouts from two decks above. He doused the glim and carefully placed it in the chest, and laid the unfinished letter under his next clean shirt.

He reached the upper deck and climbed swiftly to the larboard gangway where Dancer and Grenfell were clinging to the nettings, peering towards the glittering horizon.

Bolitho asked, 'Is it land?'

'No, Dick, a ship!' Dancer grinned at him, his face tanned and alert in the bright sunshine.

It was hard to remember the rain and bitter cold, Bolitho thought. The sea was as blue as the sky, and the crisp wind lacking in bite or menace. High above the decks the topsails and topgallants shone like pale shells, while the masthead pendant licked out towards the larboard bow like a long scarlet lance.

'Deck thar!' They all peered up at the tiny black shape of the masthead lookout. 'She bain't answerin', sir!'

It was then Bolitho realized that this was no ordinary encounter. The captain was by the quarterdeck rail, arms folded, his face in shadow, and nearby Midshipman Marrack and his signalling party were watching their halliards and the bright hoist of flags at the mainyard.

What ship?

Bolitho craned over the nettings and felt the spray touching his face and lips from the wash below. Then he saw the other vessel, a black-hulled barquentine, her sails in disarray against the blinding horizon, her masts swaying steeply in the swell.

Bolitho moved further aft and heard Mr Hope, who had the watch, exclaim, 'By God, sir, if he don't answer our signal he must be up to no good, I say!'

Verling turned towards him, his beaky nose displaying his scorn.

'If he wanted, Mr Hope, he could fly with the wind and leave us far astern within the hour.'

'Aye, sir.' Hope sounded downcast.

The captain ignored both of them.

He said, 'Pass the word to the gunner, if you please. To run out a bow chaser and fire one ball as near as he can. They're either drunk or asleep over there.'

But the solitary crash of a forward nine-pounder

45

brought nothing more than a rush of seamen from below decks in the *Gorgon* herself. The idling barquentine continued to drift, her forward sails almost aback, her big fore-and-aft canvas on main and mizzen shivering in a heat haze.

The captain snapped, 'Shorten sail and heave-to, Mr Verling! And send away the quarter boat. I am uneasy about this one.'

Calls shrilled and twittered along the maindeck, and within minutes of the captain's order *Gorgon* was going about, swinging her heavy hull round into the wind with every sail and shroud quivering and banging in confusion.

Dancer went aft to join Bolitho beneath the hammock nettings.

'D'you think –'

He stopped as Bolitho whispered, 'Keep quiet and stay here.'

Bolitho watched the boatswain mustering a boat's crew on the opposite side of the deck. With *Gorgon* hove-to and groaning into the wind Hoggett, the boatswain, was preparing the quarter boat to be hauled from astern and manhandled alongside.

The captain was speaking to Verling, his words lost in the sullen boom of flapping canvas. Then the first lieutenant turned abruptly, his nose swinging across the quarterdeck like a swivel gun.

'Pass the word! Mr Tregorren lay aft to take boarding party away!' His nose continued to move as his order was yelled forward along the maindeck. '*You two midshipmen!* Arm yourselves and accompany the fourth lieutenant!'

Bolitho touched his hat. 'Aye, aye, sir!' He nudged Dancer. 'I knew he would pick the nearest.'

Dancer grinned, the excitement bright in his eyes. 'It's good to be doing something different!'

Down by the entry port the hastily assembled oarsmen and armed seamen crowded above the blue water, their eyes outboard towards the other vessel which had drifted almost abeam and now lay about half a mile distant.

Mr Hope called, 'I can read her name, sir!' He sounded cautious after Verling's earlier sarcasm. 'She's the *City of Athens*!' He was swaying back and forth in the uncomfortable swell, a big telescope held to his eye. 'No sign of life aboard!'

Lieutenant Tregorren arrived at the entry port, his frame seeming larger and more forceful without the low-beamed gundeck to restrain it. His eyes flashed across his boarding party.

He said bluntly, 'Let no man loose off a pistol or musket by error. Be ready for anything.' His gaze settled on Bolitho and he added, 'As for you –'

He broke off as the captain's voice called from the quarterdeck rail, 'Man your boat, Mr Tregorren.' His eyes were like glass in the bright glare. 'If it's fever aboard I want no part of it. Do what you can and be lively with it.'

Bolitho watched him gravely. He did not know the captain, other than at a distance or seeing him at work with his officers. And yet he was almost certain that Captain Conway was on edge, anxious enough to speak severely to one of his lieutenants in front of the people. He flushed as the cold eyes settled on him.

'You.' The captain half lifted one hand. 'What is your name again?'

'Bolitho, sir.' It was strange that nobody ever seemed to remember a midshipman's name.

'Well, *Bolitho*, when you have quite finished your daydream, or composing a poem for your doxy, I'd be grateful if you would enter the boat!'

Several seamen lounging at the gangway chuckled, and Tregorren rasped angrily, 'If I thought you were trying to show me up!' He gave Bolitho a thrust with his palm. 'I'll deal with you later!'

Once in the quarter boat, one of *Gorgon*'s twenty-eight-foot cutters, the captain's mood, Tregorren's hostility and the discomfort of six weeks at sea were pushed from Bolitho's mind. Crowded in the stern-sheets amongst the extra men and weapons, with Tregorren's great shadow swaying over the labouring oars, he turned and glanced quickly astern. How huge and invulnerable *Gorgon* appeared from a low-hulled boat. Standing above her rippling reflection, her masts and yards stark and black against the sky, she looked a symbol of sea power.

He could tell from Dancer's expression that he shared his excitement. He looked leaner than when they had met at the Blue Posts, but tougher and more confident.

Tregorren snapped, 'Give the fellow a hail!' He was standing upright in the boat, oblivious to the lively motion as it lifted and sliced over the wave-crests.

The bowman cupped his hands. '*Ship ahoy!*' His voice seemed to echo back like an acknowledgement.

Dancer whispered, 'What d'you reckon, Dick?'

Bolitho shook his head. 'Not sure.'

He watched the barquentine's masts lifting above the sweating oarsmen, the way the booms on her main and mizzen creaked and shook without purpose.

'*Way 'nough!*'

The oars stilled and the bowman hurled a grapnel high over the vessel's bulwark.

Tregorren snapped, 'Easy now!' He stood staring up at the bulwark, uncertain, or as if he still expected somebody to appear. Then, 'Boarders away!'

The boatswain had chosen only experienced hands, and within seconds they were all up and over the sun-dried bulwark and clustered close together beneath the batlike sails.

Tregorren said, 'Mr Dancer, take the forrard hatch!' He gestured to a boatswain's mate, the one who had carried out the flogging. 'Thorne, you make certain that the main hatch is secure.' Surprisingly, he drew a pistol from his belt and cocked it carefully. '*Mr* Bolitho, and you two, will come aft to the poop with me.'

Bolitho glanced at his friend who gave a quick shrug before taking his own men to the forward hatch. Nobody was smiling now. It was like a phantom ship, deserted and neglected, her crew spirited away. He looked towards the *Gorgon* but even she seemed further away, her protection less certain.

Tregorren said harshly. 'This bloody ship stinks!' He stood above a companionway, his head on one side as he peered down into darkness. 'Anyone below?'

But there was no sound other than sea noises and the dismal creak of the unattended wheel.

Tregorren looked at Bolitho. 'Down you go.' He seized his wrist and added fiercely, 'Well, attend to your pistol, damn you!'

Bolitho drew the heavy weapon from his belt and stared at it.

The lieutenant said, 'And don't turn your back as you go down the ladder!'

Bolitho slid over the coaming and paused to allow his eyes to become used to the gloom between decks. Once below the poop he heard other shipboard sounds, and he had to tell himself they were quite normal. The sluice of water against the hull, the creak and clatter of loose gear. He could smell candle-grease and damp air, the more rancid stenches of bilge and stale food.

He heard a man yell from above, 'Nothing forrard, sir!' and relaxed very slightly. On the planks above, muffled but recognizable, Tregorren was moving this way and that, probably wondering what to do next. But he remembered Tregorren's haste to send him below first and without aid. If he was concerned about this strange, deserted vessel he was certainly indifferent to his midshipman's safety.

He pushed open a small cabin door and stooped to enter. It was so low beneath the deck beams that he had to shuffle in the darkness like a hunchback, his hands groping to stop the ship from throwing him off balance.

His fingers touched a lantern before his face. It was ice-cold.

At that moment a tiny hatch was flung open overhead and a previously concealed skylight wrenched aside. Framed in the blinding glare, Tregorren's massive head peered down at him.

'What the hell are you doing, *Mr* Bolitho?'

He fell silent, and when Bolitho turned to follow his stare he saw why.

Sprawled in one corner of the cabin was a man, or all there was left of him.

He had received a terrible head wound from cutlass or axe and had taken several more thrusts in chest and side. In the shaft of sunlight his gaze seemed to be slitted against the brightness, his eyes terrified as they fixed on Bolitho.

Tregorren said at length, 'God Almighty!' Then as Bolitho remained stockstill beside the corpse he added roughly, 'On deck with you!'

In the bright sunlight again Bolitho found that his hands were shaking badly, although when he looked at them they seemed as before.

Tregorren ordered, 'Put a hand on the wheel, Thorne. Mr Dancer, take your men to the main hold and search it. The rest of you begin to take in these damned sails!'

He turned as Dancer called, '*Gorgon*'s under way again, sir.'

'Yes.' The lieutenant was frowning with the effort of thinking. 'She'll be dropping down within hailing distance. By that time I want some answers.'

It was like putting together parts of a torn and dismembered book. Dancer's search of the barquentine's main hold revealed that she had been carrying spirits, mostly rum, but the hold, apart from a few broken and upended casks, was empty. By the starboard rail on the poop, and again on the compass box, they found dried blood and the burn marks from discharged pistols.

The solitary corpse in the cabin must have been the vessel's master, running below to arm himself, to save some valuables or merely to hide. It was not clear. What was certain was that he had been brutally murdered.

Bolitho heard Tregorren say to the boatswain's mate, 'Must've been a mutiny and the devils made off after killing the loyal seamen.'

But both of the barquentine's boats were still hoisted inboard and secured.

Then, when *Gorgon*'s great pyramid of sails was running slowly across the vessel's quarter, Heather, one of Dancer's party, discovered something else. Just aft of the main hold a ball had smashed into the timbers, and when the hull dipped across a deep trough it was possible to see where it had struck the outside of the ship. By leaning out from the shrouds Bolitho saw it shining from its jagged socket like a malevolent black eye.

Tregorren said heavily, 'Must have been a pirate of some sort. Put a shot into her when she failed to heave-to and then boarded her.' He ticked off the points on his spatulate fingers. 'Then butchered the hands and pitched 'em overboard. There are sharks a'plenty hereabouts. Then they swayed out the cargo to their own ship and cast off.'

He looked round irritably as Dancer asked, 'But why not seize the ship too, sir?'

'I was coming to that,' he replied angrily. But he did not explain further. Instead, he cupped his hands and began to bellow some of his news towards the *Gorgon*.

Across the narrowing stretch of water Bolitho heard Verling's voice through his speaking trumpet.

'Continue the search and remain under our lee.'

That was probably to give the captain time to examine his own logs and documents about local shipping. The *City of Athens* was obviously not a new vessel, and was probably familiar on the rum trade from the West Indies.

Bolitho shivered, imagining himself alone and suddenly faced with a rush of savage, stabbing boarders.

Tregorren said shortly, 'Down aft again.' He strode to the companion with Bolitho at his heels.

Even though he knew what he would see it was still a shock. Bolitho tried not to look at the dead man's face as Tregorren, after a brief hesitation, began to search his pockets. The *City of Athens'* log and charts had vanished, probably overboard, but in a corner of the littered cabin, almost hidden under a bunk, Tregorren found a canvas envelope. It was empty, but had the vessel's agent's name in Martinique clearly printed on it. It was better than nothing.

The lieutenant righted an upended chair and sat on it heavily, his head still almost brushing the deck beams. He remained in the same position for several minutes, staring at the corpse, his face dark with concentration.

Bolitho said, 'I believe there was a *third* vessel, sir. That the attackers or pirates saw *her* sail and decided to make a run for it, knowing that this one would attract first attention.'

For an instant he thought Tregorren had not heard.

Then the lieutenant said softly, 'When I require aid from you, Mr Bolitho, I will ask for it.' He looked up, his eyes in shadow. 'You may be a post-captain's son, and the grandson of a flag officer, but to me you are a *midshipman*, less than nothing in my book!'

'I – I'm sorry.' Bolitho felt himself tense with anger. 'I meant no offence.'

'Oh yes, I know your family.' Tregorren's chest was lifting with exertion and suppressed fury. 'I've seen the fine house, the tablets on the church wall! Well, *I* had no safe background to help me, and by God I'll see you get no favours in my ship, *understood*?' He swung away, controlling his voice with obvious effort. 'Now tell someone to cast down a line and haul that corpse on deck. Then have 'em clean up the cabin, it stinks like a gallow's-tip down here!'

He touched the leg of his chair. There was dried blood on it, black in the filtered sunlight.

Almost to himself he muttered, 'Probably yesterday. Otherwise the rats would have found their way in here.'

He jammed on his salt-stained hat and ducked out of the cabin.

Later, while Bolitho and Dancer waited by the

bulwark and watched the lieutenant being pulled across to *Gorgon*'s side to make his report, Bolitho told his friend something of what had happened between them.

Dancer eyed him sadly. 'I'll wager he intends to put your ideas to the captain, Dick. It would be just like him.'

Bolitho touched his arm, recalling Tregorren's last words before he had dropped into the boat.

'Keep steerage way until told what to do, and send a good lookout aloft.' He had pointed at the corpse by the wheel. 'And throw *that* overboard. It's how some of you'll end up, I shouldn't wonder.'

Bolitho looked now at the empty space where the unknown man had lain. *Callous and senseless.*

He said, 'I've a few more ideas yet.' He smiled, trying to forget his anger. 'At least I know why he dislikes *me*.'

Dancer followed his mood. 'Remember that poor cripple in the Blue Posts, Dick?' He gestured around the deck and at the handful of seamen. 'He said we would both be captains, and, by God, we have a ship of our own already!'

4

'Clear for Action!'

THE *Gorgon*'s wardroom, situated directly below the captain's great cabin, and which was approximately the same size, was packed with figures from bulkhead to stern windows. It was lined with small, white-painted cabins and used as a home and dining-space by the lieutenants, the master, the marine officers and Laidlaw, the surgeon.

But in the pink glow of sunset through the stern windows and beneath several spiralling lanterns, the wardroom was filled with almost everyone above the rank of petty officer, except those needed to work the ship.

Bolitho and Dancer found themselves a space on the larboard side by an open window and looked round hopefully for some refreshments. But if the wardroom was required to donate its space for a conference it was not apparently inclined to make its guests welcome.

For most of the day, while *Gorgon* and her small consort had ghosted along under reduced canvas,

Bolitho and Dancer had fretted and speculated about what was going to happen, and what their part would be. A boat had eventually been sent for them to rejoin *Gorgon*, the boatswain's mate, Thorne, saying with as much sarcasm as he dared, 'I *think* I can manage to take charge till you young gennlemen get back, sir.' He had served ten years with the fleet.

Now, as they waited with the other midshipmen, ignored by the lieutenants and marine officers, Bolitho and his friend watched the screen door by the trunk of the mizzen mast which pinioned the ship from poop to keel. It was like being in a theatre waiting for the principal actor to appear, or for an Assize judge to take his place and begin a trial.

Bolitho glanced around the wardroom, not for the first time. Different again from the spacious cabin overhead, it was nevertheless a palace after the midshipmen's berth and gunroom. Even the little cabin doors which left the occupants barely more room than a cupboard suggested privacy and something personal. A table and some good chairs were scattered amongst the standing figures and not jammed together against the curved and often dripping side of the orlop.

He turned and leaned over the sill, seeing the froth from the rudder very pink in the sunset, the million dancing mirrors which streamed down from the horizon. It was hard to think of murder and danger, a man being hacked to death in the trim barquentine which sailed under *Gorgon*'s lee.

Another two years and he would share a wardroom like this, Bolitho thought. One more step up the ladder.

He heard feet shuffling around him and Dancer's quick, 'Here they come!'

Verling entered first, holding the screen door aside so that Captain Beves Conway could move aft without taking his hands from behind his back.

When he reached the table Conway said, 'They may sit down if they wish.'

Bolitho watched him, fascinated. Hemmed in by his lieutenants, the warrant officers and midshipmen, he still managed to appear quite removed from all of them. He was wearing a well-pressed blue coat, its white lapels and gilt buttons as fresh as from any London tailor. Breeches and stockings equally clean and neat, and his hair was tied to the nape of his neck with a fresh twist of ribbon. Most of the midshipmen saved their ribbons for special occasions. Bolitho, for instance, had his long black hair tied above his collar with a piece of codline.

Verling said briefly, 'Pay attention. The captain wishes to address you.'

The wardroom seemed to be holding its breath, so that the sigh of sea and wind, the irregular creak of the rudder-head beneath the stern windows intruded forcefully, and Bolitho marvelled at the fact that they had sailed all four thousand miles without any real knowledge of why they were doing it.

The captain said quietly, 'I have brought you all here together to save time. You will return to your messes or your divisions when I have finished and tell the people what we are about, in your own way. Far better than a fine speech from the quarterdeck, I think.' He cleared his throat and looked at their expectant faces. 'My orders were to bring this ship to the west coast of Africa and carry out a patrol, and if necessary land seamen and marines to further those orders. In the last few years there has been a growing menace of piracy along these shores, and many fine ships have been fired on or have disappeared.'

He was speaking without emotion or excitement, and Bolitho wondered how such outward calm was possible. All these miles, with many more yet to sail, with the health and management of a raw company to deal with, the uncertainties of what he might find at the end of each voyage. It could not be so easy to command as he had imagined.

Conway added, 'Information came to the Admiralty some months ago that some of these pirates had made their base on the coast of Senegal.' For a moment his eyes settled on the untidy cluster of midshipmen. 'Which now lies less than thirty miles to lee'rd, Mr Turnbull assures me.'

The ruddy-faced sailing master smiled grimly and nodded. 'Near as dammit, sir.'

'So be it.' The brief touch of humour had gone. 'It is my duty to discover this hiding place, and my intention is then to destroy it and punish all responsible for these crimes.'

Bolitho shivered, despite the oppressive heat in the wardroom, remembering the withered corpses of some captured pirates dangling in irons outside his own town of Falmouth.

The captain said wryly, 'Naturally their lordships, in all their wisdom, chose a seventy-four for the task.'

The master and several of the older men nodded and grinned as he continued, 'A ship too deep-hulled to work close inshore and too slow to catch a pirate vessel on the high seas! However, we do now have the barquentine, which Mr Tregorren has now put into fair shape for use in the King's name.'

Several heads turned to peer at the massive lieutenant as Conway added, 'He has informed me of his observations concerning the vessel's fate, and has suggested that the attackers may have been frightened off by the appearance of another ship. As it was likely this happened yesterday, it may have been *our* topgallants which the pirates saw. If it was near this time, and allowing for wind and current, the *City of Athens* may well have been cloaked in dusk while we still held the sunset as we do now.'

He shrugged, as if tired of speculation. 'Be that as it may, they robbed a peaceful merchantman and no doubt threw the crew to the sharks, or so terrified the survivors that they will hang with their captors when we take them, as take them we must!'

Verling took the hint and asked, 'Questions?'

Dewar, the major of marines, asked bluntly, 'What sort of opposition may we expect, sir?'

The captain eyed him for several seconds. 'There is a small island off the coast which was first discovered about four hundred years ago and which has been occupied by the Dutch, the French, even ourselves for most of the time. It is well sited for defence from the shore. About a mile or so out in shark-infested waters –' He paused, his eyes impatient. '*Well?*'

Hope, the fifth lieutenant, asked lamely, 'Why from the shore, sir?'

Surprisingly, Captain Conway offered a small smile. 'A good question, Mr Hope, I am glad someone was paying attention.' He ignored Hope's flush of pleasure and Tregorren's scowl. 'The reason is simple. The island has always been used for gathering slaves for sale and shipment to the Americas.' He sensed the sudden uneasiness amongst his officers and snapped, 'It is a foul trade but not illegal. The slavers assemble their victims for the captivery, and any who do not measure up to the traders' needs are disposed of to the sharks. This "convenience" also prevents friends or relations from saving the wretches from a living hell elsewhere.'

Major Dewar eyed his marine lieutenant and muttered fiercely, 'By God, we'll show 'em, eh? I don't care a fig about slavery one way or t'other, but any pirate is vermin as far as I'm concerned.'

Dancer said softly, 'My father has often said that slavery and piracy go hand in hand. The one section preys on the other, or they work together against authority when it suits them.'

Little Eden murmured excitedly, 'Wait t-till they see the *Gorgon* c-coming for them, eh?' He rubbed his hands. 'J-just you w-wait!'

Verling barked, 'Silence there!'

The captain glanced around the wardroom. 'We will lie-to and then close the land tomorrow. It is a dangerous coastline, and I have no desire to leave the keel on some reef or other. Our new consort will lead the approach, and landing parties will be detailed at first light.' He moved towards the door. 'Carry on, Mr Verling.'

The first lieutenant waited for the door to shut and said, 'Return to your messes.' He sought out a master's mate. 'Mr Ivey, you are to take charge of the *City of Athens* for the night. I suggest you call away a boat immediately.'

Dancer sighed. 'Tregorren steals your ideas, Dick, and now they've taken our first command.' He grinned. 'But I think I feel a mite safer in this fat old lady!'

Eden grinned. 'I can s-smell f-food!' He hurried from the wardroom, his feet guided by his stomach.

'We may as well go too, Dick.'

They both turned as Tregorren's voice followed them to the gundeck. 'Belay that! I've work for you two. Get aloft to the fore t'ga'n's'l yard and examine the splicing those lazy devils were supposed to be doing there while we were aboard the prize.' He regarded them calmly. 'Not too dark for you, is it? Or too *dangerous* mebbee?'

Dancer opened his mouth to answer but Bolitho said, 'Aye, aye, sir.'

The lieutenant called after them, 'No skimping now!'

On the darkening gangway by the weather shrouds Bolitho said quietly, 'I wonder if I'm always to be cursed by a fear of heights?'

They stood looking up at the black criss-cross of rigging, the braced foretopsail yard, and the one above it, deep pink in the dying light which had already gone from the decks below.

Dancer said, 'I'll go, Dick. He'll never know.'

Bolitho smiled grimly. '*He'll* know, Martyn. It would be just what he wanted.' He removed his coat and hat and wedged them under a rack of boarding pikes. 'Let's be about it then. At least it will give us an appetite!'

Aft by the big double wheel the helmsmen watched the flickering compass light and eased the spokes very slightly, their bare feet planted on the deck as if they were part of it.

The officer of the watch moved restlessly along the weather side, glancing occasionally to the opposite beam where the barquentine's solitary lantern made a small glow on the sea's face.

From beneath the poop Captain Conway strode past the wheel, his hands behind him, his body angled to the deck.

The senior helmsman nudged his mate and called, 'Steady as she goes, sir! Sou'-east by south!'

The captain nodded and waited for the lieutenant on watch to hurry discreetly to the lee side and leave him the privacy he needed for his nightly walk.

Up and down the weather side, his shoes tapping on the smooth planking. Once he paused to glance through the mainmast rigging to two shadowy figures high up on the foretopgallant yard, like birds on a perch.

But he soon forgot them as he continued pacing and thinking of tomorrow.

On this particular morning all hands were called early from their hammocks to an even hastier meal of oatmeal gruel and toasted ship's biscuit, washed down with a tankard of ale.

As one elderly seaman commented gloomily, 'To get such a good fill-up this early means the cap'n's expectin' trouble!'

Then, as the first hint of dawn showed itself in the eastern sky, and the cooks doused the galley fires, the pipe came from aft, '*Hands to quarters! Hands to quarters and clear for action!*'

Urged on by the frenzied tattoo of the drummer boys as they beat to quarters from the poop, by the additional shouts and threats from warrant officers and senior hands alike, *Gorgon's* company went into one more drill, one which they had practised and practised until their limbs had ached through sleet and boiling sun alike until they knew where every man, each piece of equipment, every line and halliard should be when the ship was called to action.

Some of the seasoned men took greater care this time, perhaps they expected that today's drill meant more than it showed. Others, and the very young like Eden, went to their stations like excited children, unquenched even by curses from exasperated lieutenants and threats from their companions.

Down on the lower gundeck Bolitho felt his own heart beating faster than usual. In the near-darkness of the low-beamed deck he could see seamen ducking and clambering around each great thirty-two-pounder, heard their bare feet grating on the sand which some ship's boys had sprinkled liberally around the decks to stop them slipping or falling during the drill.

Some light filtered down from the companion on the upper deck, and he was able to see the gun crews checking their gear and casting off the breechings to check the training tackles and test their handspikes.

High overhead they could hear the muffled squeal of blocks as nets were rigged above the deck and its guns to protect the men underneath from falling spars and broken rigging. How many times had they done it over the four thousand miles?

He felt men hurrying past, guided by the boatswain's thick voice. Screens were still being torn down, chests, tables and unwanted clutter being taken below to the orlop.

Tregorren's voice boomed in the gloom, 'Lively, you scum! It's taken far too long already!'

On the lower gundeck, apart from the mass of seamen needed to work the double battery of thirty-two-pounders, were two lieutenants, Tregorren being in charge, and Mr Wellesley, the ship's junior lieutenant, his assistant, and four midshipmen. The latter were evenly placed along the various divisions of guns, and were supposed to relay orders, fire independently if need be, and carry messages to the quarterdeck. Bolitho and Dancer shared the larboard side, and a sulky youth named Pearce and little Eden had the starboard battery.

Halfway along the deck Tregorren stood with his back to the mainmast trunk, arms folded, his head bent down to peer along his domain. Nearby a marine sentry stood by the companion ladder, as did others at every hatch, so that in the event of battle he could prevent the less brave from running below to hide.

Wellesley, the sixth lieutenant, hurried down the larboard side, his sword flapping against his thigh as he paused by each gun captain just long enough to hear the man snap, 'Ready, sir!'

At last it was all still, and only the gentle heave of the deck, the regular creak of tackles as the guns tugged or nudged to the ship's roll broke the silence.

Bolitho could smell the tension, the men around him, the hull deeper still under his feet. He tried not to think of the midshipmen's berth on the orlop, the after cockpit as it was called, which too had been transformed. There now would be the surgeon and his assistants. Lanterns lit, instruments gleaming in the open cases. Just as they had done it to Captain Conway's orders on countless occasions.

Tregorren yelled, 'Mr Wellesley! What kept you?'

The sixth lieutenant scuttled towards him and almost went sprawling across a ring-bolt.

He gasped, 'Lower battery cleared for action, sir!'

On the deck above they heard a whistle and someone calling, 'Cleared for action, sir!'

Tregorren swore savagely. 'Beaten us again, damn them!' He added harshly, 'Mr Eden! Pass the word, at the double!'

Eden returned, his breath wheezing as he reported, 'The first lieutenant's compliments, sir, and the ship cleared for action in twelve minutes.' He hesitated. 'But –'

'But what?'

The boy gulped. 'It took us longer than anyone else, sir.'

More orders were being piped, the calls of the boatswain's mates shrilling like birds on a Norfolk fen.

'Open ports!'

Bolitho leaned forward to restrain one of the gun crews. It was stiflingly hot between decks, but he knew that every port should open as one, here and on the deck above. As the port lids were hoisted upward he felt the cooler air fanning around him, saw the men nearest him take on personality and meaning, their bodies stripped to the waist and shining faintly in the strange dawn light. He glanced aft and saw Dancer give him a quick wave.

During the morning watch *Gorgon* had altered course slightly and was now steering east-south-east, the wind having shifted to the north and held there. The hull tilted and felt steady, and with the wind coming across the larboard quarter, Bolitho's section of guns was pointing high and free from spray. He saw the lively whitecaps, some strange fish leaping like birds along the ship's wash and keeping level with their slow approach. By leaning out and around a gun muzzle he saw a darker shape on the water and guessed it to be the *City of Athens*. He tried to guess what was happening on deck. The prize vessel was obviously leaving her station downwind of her protector and was beating across their line of advance to place herself between *Gorgon* and the land, wherever that was.

A young seaman asked, 'Can you see the land, sir?' He was a good-looking youth who had come from Devon to join the ship. During the night watches and the sweating drill at this same gun he had explained that all his family had worked for their local squire. A hard man, and one taken with abusing the daughters of his tenant farmers and labourers.

That was all he had confided, but Bolitho guessed it likely that he had given the squire a beating and then run to join a ship, any ship, to escape punishment.

Bolitho replied, 'Very near, I'd say, Fairweather. I can see some sea-birds now. Coming out to take a look at us, I shouldn't wonder.'

'Silence on the gundeck!' Tregorren's anger seemed to spread itself to officers and seamen alike.

Someone gave a yelp of pain as a gun captain used a rope's end, and from right aft Wellesley's rather ineffectual voice called, 'Take that man's name, I say!'

Nobody knew what man, or to whom the order was directed, and Bolitho guessed that the lieutenant was merely trying to avoid Tregorren's tongue.

It was strange how cut off from the rest of the ship it felt. More light was painting the sea in black and yellow patterns, but the horizon and sky were still as one. The square gunport cut in the ship's massive oak side was like a picture, Bolitho thought, but as the light strengthened and spilled down the long barrel of the thirty-two-pounder they all seemed to become part of it. Colour stood out now inside the gundeck. The dark red paint which was used on the ship's side, and much of the deck beneath them, showed itself for the first time. It was there to disguise the blood of dead and wounded men, everyone knew that. Bolitho glanced down the sloping deck to the opposite side. Those open gunports were still in darkness, broken here and there by some leaping feathers of spray or a crest breaking close to the hull.

He looked towards Tregorren who was speaking quietly with Jehan, the gunner, silent in his felt slippers which he always wore to prevent striking sparks when he was working in his beloved magazine. He vanished down the nearest ladder by the marine sentry, and Bolitho wondered if Dancer was thinking of the fact that the most dangerous mass of gunpowder in time of action was directly beneath his feet.

There was something like a sigh as the first sheen of sunlight filtered across the water and through each open port.

Bolitho leaned on the gun's breech and watched it transform the horizon into something real and solid. The land.

Fairweather asked excitedly, 'Be that Africa?'

The gun captain showed his uneven teeth. 'Don't matter to you where it be, lad. Just attend to old Freda 'ere and keep 'er fed, no matter what! That's all you need to know!'

A midshipman pattered down from the next deck and sought out Tregorren.

'Mr Verling's compliments, sir.' It was a midshipman named Knibb, a boy as small and as young as

Eden, but for a month's difference. 'And we will not be loading just yet.'

Tregorren snapped, 'What's happening then?'

Knibb blinked around him, seeking out his friends. 'The masthead has reported sighting two vessels at anchor around the point, sir.'

His confidence was growing, aided by the knowledge that every shadowy figure was listening to him, trying to discover what was going on in that other world above.

'Our captain has ordered the barquentine to make more sail and investigate, sir.'

The gun captain beside Bolitho was explaining to his crew. 'I know these 'ere waters, lads. Reefs an' shoals everywhere. Our cap'n'll 'ave two good leadsmen in the chains b'now, takin' regular soundins. *Feelin'* our way inshore.'

Bolitho did not hear them. He was thinking of the deserted barquentine, the dead man in her cabin. He wondered if Tregorren's obvious ill-humour was because he had not been given command of the *City of Athens*.

The third lieutenant, Tregorren's immediate superior, had been sent instead, and was assisted by Grenfell, the senior midshipman. If all went well, this little piece of extra responsibility would see the midshipman well on his way to promotion. Bolitho was glad for him, if envious of his freedom. Grenfell had done all he could to make him, and the awkward newcomers in his midst, welcome. It was not unusual for midshipmen in Grenfell's place to act like little tyrants.

Two ships at anchor, Knibb had said. Pirates or slavers? Both would get a shock when *Gorgon* made her entrance.

Feet tramped dully overhead and Bolitho heard the squeak of blocks as once again the yards were trimmed, the sails reset while the ship altered course.

He moved inboard and rested his hands on the great capstan which was used for hoisting heavy spars or boats to their allotted positions and listened to Tregorren's harsh voice as he spoke to Wellesley and Midshipman Pearce.

Beyond them the open ports were more sharply defined, and for a moment Bolitho thought that the light was playing tricks on him. The land was probing out to greet them, which was impossible, for he could see it on his own side. He recalled suddenly what the captain had said about an island. This must be it, with the ship steering into a great arrowhead of water between it and the mainland. The anchored ships must be right ahead and invisible to both gundecks.

Tregorren was saying, 'Look, there's a fort of sorts on the island. Must be as old as bloody Moses.' He chuckled. 'Wait till you cast your eyes on some of these black lasses. They're beautiful, like –' He got no further.

Bolitho had seen what looked like a dolphin skipping across the lively inshore current, and then he heard the far off boom of an explosion. The line of breaking crests vanished, and there was a chorus of shouts and curses as a great ball slammed down hard alongside the hull.

The old gun captain shouted with disbelief, 'The devils 'ave fired on *us*, be God!'

The whole ship came alive to confused orders and the blare of a marine's trumpet. Tackles squeaked and gun trucks began to move overhead, and then came the cry, 'All guns load and prepare to run out! Starboard battery will engage first!'

Tregorren stared at the messenger's breeches, very white on the companion ladder, apparently unable to believe what he had heard.

Then with a grunt he bellowed, '*All load!* Stand by on the starboard battery!'

The seaman called Fairweather followed Bolitho to the opposite side as with sudden haste the bare-backed figures began to ram home their bulky cartridges and wads, while each gun captain selected a ball from the garlands, feeling it, testing its shape and even finish before allowing it to be rammed and wadded into his waiting gun.

Hand by hand shot up, and every eye was on the burly lieutenant.

'All loaded, sir!'

'*Run out!*'

They threw themselves on to the tackles and hauled the lumbering guns to the open ports, each truck squealing and protesting like a hog going to market. The guns remained in deep shadow along the starboard side, but the ancient fortress, as it showed itself to each breathless crew, was clear to see. Its rough walls were like gold in the frail light, its shape merging with the rocks which supported it.

Above the ramparts Bolitho saw several dark

smudges which he took for an instant to be hovering clouds of mosquitoes.

He heard a seaman mutter between his teeth, 'Them devils is heatin' shot, sir! They got furnaces goin' right the way along!'

Tregorren snarled, 'I'll flog the next man to speak!' But he sounded anxious.

As well he might, Bolitho thought. His father had told him often enough what heated shot could do to a tinder-dry hull with all its top-hamper of tarred rigging and canvas.

A voice yelled, 'Stand by to starboard! Maximum elevation and fire on the uproll!'

A petty officer jabbed a seaman on the shoulder so that he jumped as if he had been shot.

'Wind yer neckcloth round yer ears, man, less you want to be deaf all yer life!'

He winked at Bolitho. The warning had probably been for his benefit, but even midshipmen were allowed some respect.

'*Stand by!*'

The ship tilted to wind and rudder, and by each gun its captain was crouching inboard, his eye along every black muzzle towards the sky and the fortress.

'*Fire!*'

5

Change of Fortune

WITH the order to open fire being yelled from deck to deck, each gun captain thrust his slow-match to the vent and jumped aside. A split second, and yet to Bolitho, who stood between a pair of thirty-two-pounders, it seemed like an age. A long-drawn-out moment when everything was crystal-clear and unmoving, as in a painting. The barebacked seamen crouching at tackles or holding handspikes. Individual gun captains, grim-faced and concentrating only on their own ports and aim. And through each square port the sunlight on the fortress, the sky very pale without even a puff of cloud.

And then everything changed. The lower gundeck exploded to the thunder of cannon fire, the hull and timbers bucking as if caught beneath an avalanche. Gun by gun crashed inboard on its tackles, its crew running to sponge out, to ram home a charge and another gleaming ball.

Taken by the wind, the dense clouds of smoke

drifted away from the hull, shutting out the fortress, masking the sky in brown fog.

Tregorren was yelling, 'Stop your vents! Sponge out! Load!'

But his voice seemed to be coming through a curtain, the first broadside having rendered eardrums and minds almost senseless.

But the effect of firing the starboard battery was plain to see. The first nervousness was gone, instead there was a sort of wildness as gun crews peered at each other, grinned and gestured like children. It was not just another drill, it was real, and they were firing in earnest.

'*Run out!*'

Once more the trucks squeaked on the deck, the crews hurling themselves on their tackles to be first through the open ports.

Bolitho heard Wellesley say excitedly, 'They'll pipe another tune now, by heaven!'

Tregorren rasped, 'Whoever *they* may be, dammit!'

In the pause, as each crew peered along the angled muzzles, Bolitho heard the clatter of movement from the deck above. *Gorgon* must make a brave sight if there was anyone to care, he thought. Under shortened sail, no doubt, her guns bared to the early sunlight, she must be heading close inshore. He did not even know who had fired on the ship, or why, and he was surprised to discover that it did not seem to matter. In these brief minutes the men around him, the ship around all of them, had become one.

'Stand by! As you bear!' The suspense was breath-stopping. '*Fire!*'

Again the hull shook like a mad thing, the planking jarring under the feet as the guns crashed inboard, their smoke belching like a curtain beyond the ports.

Eden was cheering, despite several angry glances from Tregorren, and some of the seamen were actually laughing.

Dancer called, 'I hope they can see what we are about on the quarterdeck! We could be shooting at the sky!'

He winced as something jarred against the hull, followed immediately by a chorus of shouts from overhead.

Bolitho nodded towards him. It was a direct hit. They, whoever they were, had struck back.

Somewhere a pump began to clatter, and he guessed that a heated ball must have penetrated the timbers and water was needed to quench it before the wood took light.

A seaman near him gestured towards the deckhead. 'Give they lazy dogs summat to do, eh?'

But nobody laughed, and Bolitho saw Wellesley rubbing his chin in quick nervous movements as if he was unable to believe that someone should dare to fire at a King's ship.

'All loaded, sir!'

A messenger appeared on the companion ladder, his voice shrill. 'We are going about, sir! Prepare to engage with the larboard side!' He vanished.

Fairweather peered at Bolitho, his teeth white in the eddying smoke. 'We'm hitting 'em proper, eh, sir? Giving t'other guns a chance!'

The gun captain darted a quick glance at the breechings and snapped. 'They've got us beat. We're runnin' away, you soft fool!'

Bolitho saw the amazement on Fairweather's face and felt the gun captain's blunt words moving to the other men nearby.

Tregorren strode past, his head dipping between the massive beams.

'Stand to your guns! Prepare to run out!' He paused and glared at Bolitho. 'What th' hell are you staring at?'

'We're coming about, sir.' He kept his voice steady, aware that there was more gunfire from the far distance. Whoever commanded the fortress had plenty of artillery.

'What a *masterly* appraisal, Mr Bolitho!' Tregorren gripped a deckhead beam as *Gorgon* began to tilt steeply, the sea lifting towards the open ports as she swung heavily into the wind. 'Was the din of battle too much for you?'

'No, sir.' He met his hostility and added, 'I think we may have been too close inshore. That fortress has our exact range.'

Men, who seconds earlier had been hurrying to the opposite side, paused to watch. The towering bulk of the lieutenant and the slim midshipman, angled to the deck, their arms at their sides like antagonists meeting for a duel.

Wellesley said nervously, 'The captain knows best.'

Tregorren stared at him. 'Do you *have* to explain to a midshipman?' He looked from one to the other. 'Now stand to your guns!'

But the order to fire the larboard was not given. Instead there was a long and uncertain silence, broken only by the occasional movement of seamen on the upper deck, the twitter of calls as the hands went to braces and halliards for altering course.

The gun captain near Bolitho said darkly, 'Told you. Cap'n's standin' out to sea. Just as well, if you asks me.'

During the long and tiring gun drills Bolitho had never found time to consider how cut-off this deck could become. Now, as seamen and their officers stood or lounged beside the ports, he felt a growing sense of apprehension and uncertainty. He could tell from the slant of the sun that the ship was heading away from the land, but apart from that there was nothing to break the frustrating sense of being quite apart from the world above.

'Secure guns!' The messenger's white breeches caught the filtered sunlight on the ladder. 'All officers lay aft, if you please, sir!'

Bolitho said to Dancer, 'I think the captain has been worried all along, Martyn.'

Dancer looked at him grimly. 'But surely he would not run from a damned pirate?'

'Better than be left swimming without a ship, eh?' Bolitho tried to cheer him up. 'I know which I'd rather have.'

But if the lower gundeck was remote and as before, the quarterdeck was not. Bolitho stood blinking in the harsh glare, seeing the two great holes in the main topsail, a streak of scarlet on the planking to mark where a man had fallen, or died. He stared over the rail and saw the land shimmering in a blinding haze. Already the island and its fortress had merged with the mainland and the anchored ships quite lost from sight around the same point which they had so confidently rounded a few hours earlier. Of the barquentine there was no sign at all.

Dancer asked anxiously, 'Where is the *City of Athens*, do you think?'

Little Eden said, 'She's s-standing off t-to keep an eye on the d-devils.'

Dancer nodded. 'Bit of luck getting hold of her.'

They fell silent as Verling dismissed the hands from the quarterdeck nine-pounders and beckoned the other officers to close around him. He appeared as irritable as ever, Bolitho thought, his beaky nose checking who was present and who was yet to arrive.

Captain Conway crossed from the weather side and stood by the quarterdeck rail looking down at the eighteen-pounders below him, their crews checking their equipment and refilling the shot garlands.

There was a rank smell of powder in the air, of heated metal and charred wood.

Verling said, 'All present, sir.'

The captain turned and regarded them thoughtfully, his back against the rail, his palms resting on the polished wood.

'We are standing offshore and will anchor further along the coast. As you know, we were fired on, and fired on with a confidence I dislike.' He spoke calmly and unhurriedly, with less emotion than when he had awarded a flogging. 'The enemy is well prepared, and our bombardment, such as it was, made no impression. But I had to be certain. To gain some knowledge of what we are against.'

Bolitho could tell from the expressions of some of those nearby, who had been on the upper deck throughout the brief engagement, that there was something more to come.

Captain Conway continued in the same tone, 'Some months ago it was reported that one of our brigs, a new vessel which was employed in these waters, was overdue and therefore presumed lost. There had been some foul weather, and several merchantmen were also wrecked.' He glanced up at the masthead pendant, his eyes shining in the glare. 'When we rounded the point this morning the *City of Athens* was well in the lead. The lookouts reported sighting two vessels at anchor. There may have been more under the island's protection.' His voice hardened for the first time. 'But one of them was the missing brig, His Majesty's Ship *Sandpiper* of fourteen guns. Because of her, the *City of Athens* must have imagined that all was well, that *Sandpiper*'s captain had already done our work for us.'

Dancer gave a gasp as he added, 'The brig was the bait which we, but for our prize, would have taken. We would have laid under the guns of the fortress, and without the speed and agility to beat clear, would have been destroyed. As it was, the barquentine was hit several times. I doubt if any of her people survived.'

There was absolute silence. Bolitho was remembering the din on the lower gundeck, the importance and excitement they had all felt. He recalled the unsmiling face of Midshipman Grenfell, a face which had hidden a warmer and kinder nature than many imagined. And it had all happened without a word being passed from the quarterdeck. It would have changed nothing, could have done nothing to help. And yet . . .

The captain added slowly, 'When we took the *City of Athens*, Mr Tregorren suggested that the pirates made off upon sighting another vessel. It now seems very possible that the other sail was ours, and the reasons for the pirate's haste was that he did not want to be seen for what he is! A captured British man-o'-war. Imagine, gentleman, what havoc he may have been wreaking in *our country's name*?' He spat out the words like poison. 'No master of any peaceful vessel would challenge a ship so obviously British and in the King's service! That is not piracy, it is cold-blooded murder!'

Mr Verling nodded. 'It would be simple, sir. Whoever commands these scum has a sharp mind to attend him!'

The captain did not seem to hear. 'Some of our prize crew may have survived.' He glanced down at the dried blood by his feet. 'We may never know. However, our next task is to seize the brig and discover all we can of what is happening.'

Bolitho looked at the others. *Seize the brig.* Just like that.

'A cutting-out operation must be done tonight. No moon, and the weather favours us at present. The marines will provide a distraction. But I want that vessel retaken, the shame she has been made to endure and promote wiped out!'

He turned as the surgeon appeared on the ladder. 'Well?'

'The lookout died, sir.' Laidlaw's hooded eyes were expressionless. 'Broke his back.'

'I see.' The captain turned to the silent officers. 'The lookout was the one who first sighted *Sandpiper*. The balls which passed close above us from the battery ashore must have thrown him to the deck.'

Bolitho watched the surgeon for some sign, knowing he was remembering that same lookout was the man who had been flogged.

The captain licked his lips. It was very hot on the quarterdeck, with the worst of the day yet to come.

He said, 'Mr Verling will give you your instructions. There will be two boats for the cutting-out. More would lessen our chances.' He walked away adding, 'Carry on.'

Verling watched him go. 'Two lieutenants and three midshipmen will take charge of the attack.' He eyed Tregorren coldly. 'You will command. Take only trained hands. This is no work for ploughmen.'

Eden whispered, 'What does it m-mean, Dick?' He looked very small beside the others.

The sulky midshipman named Pearce said, 'We board the brig in the darkness and cut 'em down before they return the compliment!' He added harshly, 'Poor John Grenfell. We grew up together in the same town.'

Verling said, 'Return to your duties. The hands

can fall out from quarters and secure. Keep 'em busy, I want no bleating and sobbing for what has happened.'

They began to break up, each man wrapped in his own thoughts on the suddenness of death.

Tregorren said, 'Thirty men will be needed –'

He hesitated as Midshipman Pearce called, 'I'd like to volunteer, sir.'

Tregorren regarded him calmly. 'Mr Grenfell was a friend of yours. I had forgotten. A pity that.'

Bolitho watched him, sickened. Despite all that had happened, even the sudden likelihood of his own injury or death, Tregorren still found delight in taunting the grim-faced Pearce.

The lieutenant said abruptly, 'Request denied.' His eyes settled on Eden. '*You* will be one of the lucky midshipmen.' He smiled as Eden paled. 'A real chance to prove yourself.'

Bolitho said, 'He is the youngest, sir. Some of us have had more experience and . . .' He faltered, seeing the trap opening.

Tregorren shook one finger. 'I forgot about that, too. That our Mr Bolitho is always afraid that someone else will steal his thunder, deny him of honour, so that his high-and-mighty family might frown a bit!'

'That is a *lie*, sir. And unfair!'

Tregorren shrugged. 'Is it? No matter. You are also going, *and* the clever Mr Dancer.' He put his huge hands on his hips and looked at each in turn. 'The first lieutenant said only trained hands should be detailed. But we need experienced midshipmen for handling the ship. On a cutting-out raid we only require the right number!'

He took out his pocket watch. 'I want the full party mustered in an hour. Mr Hope will be my subordinate. Report to him when you are ready.'

Dancer said bitterly, 'Better Hope than Wellesley. He is as weak as watered milk.'

They walked along the weather gangway, thinking of Grenfell and the others who had been lost in the shattered barquentine.

Eden said fiercely, 'I – I'm n-not afraid! R-really I'm not!' He looked at them wretchedly, his eyes filling his face. 'It's just that I d-don't want to go with Mr T-Tregorren! H-he'll be the d-death of us all!'

Dancer looked down at him and tried to smile. 'We'll be with you, Tom. It may not be too bad.' He turned suddenly to Bolitho. 'What *is* it like, Dick? You've done this sort of thing before.'

Bolitho stared across the nettings towards the misty hump of land and the glittering expanse of water.

'It's quick. Everything depends on surprise.'

He did not look at them. What could he say? Tell them of the fearful cries and curses of men fighting with cutlasses and knives, with axes and pikes. Of the touch of an enemy, the feel of his breath and his hatred. It was not like a sea fight, with the enemy just another ship. It was people. Flesh and blood.

Dancer said quietly, 'I can tell from your silence. Let us hope we are lucky.'

Down on the orlop they found Pearce and two other midshipmen restoring the chests and well-used chairs to their proper places, the surgeon's mates having removed their instruments and medicines as soon as the secure was piped.

In its place against one of *Gorgon*'s great frames was Grenfell's chest, his best hat and dirk hanging above it.

Pearce said, 'He always said he'd never rate lieutenant. He never will now.'

Bolitho looked round as Midshipman Marrack entered, impeccable as ever in a clean shirt.

Marrack said shortly, 'Leave his gear alone. There may still be a chance.' He threw his coat on a chair and added, 'You should have seen her go. The *City of Athens* never stood a chance. She was actually shortening sail to close the brig when the fortress battery took her.' He stared at nothing. 'She took fire and then turned turtle. I saw some of our people swimming. Then the sharks came.' He could not go on.

Dancer looked at Bolitho. 'I remember reading something about the *Sandpiper*.

Marrack said, 'One thing is certain. Our captain will never allow a King's ship to remain in enemy hands, no matter what it costs to recover her.' He reached into his chest and took out a leather case. 'Take my pistols, Dick. They're better than any others aboard. My father gave them to me.' He turned away, as if annoyed at showing a softer side to his nature. 'See what confidence I have in you?'

The small servant scuttled into the berth. 'Beg pardon, sirs, but the fourth lieutenant is lookin' for you, and yellin' murder!'

'That Tregorren!' Dancer was unusually bitter.

'I agree with little Tom here. The damned bully is too full of himself for my liking!'

They made for the companion ladder, and only then realized that Eden was still by the side. He was staring at Grenfell's chest and his dirk which swung easily to the ship's movements.

Bolitho said gently, 'Come on, Tom. There's a lot to be done before sunset.'

To himself he added, *and after.*

6

Face to Face

'EASY there! Watch your stroke!' Hope, the *Gorgon*'s
fifth lieutenant, hissed in the darkness, craning forward from the sternsheets as if to seek out the noise.

Bolitho crouched beside him and turned to peer
astern. Only an occasional feather of white spray or a
trailing glow of phosphorescence around the oars
betrayed the position of the other cutter. It was very
dark, and after the cloudless day, surprisingly cold.
Which was just as well, he thought, for they had
come a long way. The boats had been lowered and
manned before dusk, and while *Gorgon* made more
sail and went about to leave them to their own
resources they had settled down to a long, steady pull
towards the slab of headland.

When darkness had arrived it had been sudden,
like the fall of a curtain, and Bolitho found himself
wondering what was going on in the lieutenant's
mind. It was a far cry indeed from the time when he
had thrown open the door of the Blue Posts at
Portsmouth and bellowed at the midshipmen. He

remembered what Grenfell had said then about Hope's worries of promotion. The memory saddened him. Grenfell was dead, and Hope would indeed be moving up a place when the captain chose to accept that the lieutenant who had been in charge of the *City of Athens* was also killed.

Eden was leaning against him, his head lowered almost to the gunwale.

Bolitho said quietly, 'Still a way to go yet, Tom.'

It was an eerie sensation. The cutter thrusting jerkily across the inshore currents, the oars rising and falling on either beam like pale bones, their usual noise muffled by rags and thick layers of grease.

Ahead of the boat there was a darker wedge to show the division between sea and sky, and Bolitho thought he could smell the earth, sense its nearness.

In the bows, bent over the stem and a vicious-looking swivel gun, was a leadsman, his boat's lead and line sounding the way above sandbars and hidden rocks.

Turnbull, the master, had explained to the two lieutenants that it was best to creep right inshore, so that once around the headland they would lie somewhere between the beach and the anchored ships.

It had all sounded so easy. Not now, as a man caught his foot in a cutlass and set it clattering across the bottom-boards, and Hope snarled, 'God, Rogers, I'll have you beaten senseless if you make another sound!'

Bolitho looked at his profile, a shadow against the oars' spray alongside. A lieutenant. A man who knew that Tregorren was following close astern, depending on his ability to lead the way. Thirty men. For a press-gang, or for manning a couple of heavy guns, it was ample. For taking a ship against odds, and without surprise, it was disaster.

A strong eddy pushed the hull aside, so that the coxswain had to use his strength at the tiller to bring it back on course. The air felt different again and the sea across the larboard beam looked livelier.

Bolitho ventured, 'We are round the headland, sir.'

Hope swung on him and then said, 'Yes. *You'd* know, of course. You must have grown up with rocks like these in Cornwall.' He seemed to be studying him in the darkness. 'But a long pull yet.'

Bolitho hesitated, unwilling to break the little contact between them. 'Will the marines attack the battery, sir?'

'Some mad scheme like that.' Hope wiped his face as spray lanced into the boat. 'The captain will tack as close as he dares to the seaward end of the island and pretend to attempt a landing. Plenty of noise. Major Dewar will be good at that, he's got plenty to say in the wardroom!'

The whisper came back along the oarsmen. 'Vessel at anchor on th' starboard bow, sir!'

Hope nodded. 'Steer a point or so to larboard.' He twisted round to make sure the other boat was following. 'That must be the first of 'em. The brig is anchored beyond her, a couple of cables yet.'

Someone groaned, more worried apparently at the prospect of pulling a heavy oar for another four hundred yards than the possible closeness of death.

'Watch out!' The bowman dropped his lead and line and seized a boathook.

The oars went into momentary confusion as something large and black, like a sleeping whale, loomed over the cutter, banging into the blades and making what seemed like a tremendous noise.

Eden murmured shakily, 'It's p-part of the b-barquentine, Dick!'

'Yes.'

Bolitho could smell the charred timbers, could even recognise a part of the *City of Athens*' taffrail before it lurched away into the darkness.

The unexpected appearance of part of the wreck had quite an effect on the seamen. There was something like a low growl, and tired though they were, the oarsmen started putting an extra power into their stroke.

Hope said softly, 'These are seasoned hands, Bolitho. They have been in *Gorgon* together for a long while and had plenty of friends aboard the prize.' He stiffened as the sweeping masts and yards of an anchored vessel passed slowly abeam. 'There she goes. Nary a damn sound.'

Bolitho peered at the darkened ship. Moored alongside the *Gorgon* she would look dwarfed. Out here, and from the cutter, she appeared enormous.

Hope was thinking aloud. 'Small frigate most likely. Not English. Too much rake on her masts.' He sounded completely absorbed. 'This devil has gathered quite a fleet, it seems.'

'Ease the stroke!' The coxswain whispered fiercely, 'Here comes t'other one!'

Hope rose to his feet, steadying himself on Bolitho's shoulder. Bolitho could feel the power of his grip, could imagine his anxieties at this moment.

Hope said, 'If only I could look at my watch.'

The coxswain grinned. 'Might as well send the devils a signal, sir.'

'Aye.' Hope sighed. 'Let's pray that Major Dewar and his bullocks are punctual.'

He peered over the gunwale, watching the swirl of the current, testing the wind against his face.

He seemed satisfied. 'Easy all!'

The oars rose dripping from the water and stayed motionless, the cutter moving steadily ahead in complete silence.

Bolitho saw the anchored brig for the first time. Swinging stern-on, her gilded cabin windows showing more brightly than the lower hull as she pivoted very slowly away from the land.

He could just make out her two masts and furled sails, the blacker angles of her shrouds, before they too merged with the night.

Bolitho tried to put himself in the place of those aboard. They had fought and captured the barquentine, robbed her holds and killed her crew. At the sight of a large man-of-war they had sheered off and come back here to count their gains. *Gorgon*'s appearance offshore would have caused a lot of speculation, but under the guns of the old fortress they would have felt secure enough. The fortress had been here for a few hundred years, the captain had said. It had changed hands several times by treaty, or because of a trading agreement, but had never been taken by force. Just a few men at those carefully sited guns, some heated shot, and the rest was easy. Even if Captain Conway had commanded several small, agile ships, and ten times as many men, the fortress would still have held the key to victory. And in time of peace it was doubtful if either the Admiralty or the men of Parliament would be prepared to condone a full-scale siege on this tiny pinprick of Africa, with all the losses entailed. Equally, they would expect Captain Conway to do something. To recapture the brig for a beginning.

A shaft of silver ran up the brig's foremast shrouds, and Hope snapped, 'The anchor watch in the bows! Checking the cable!'

The lantern's beam died away just as quickly.

The drift of the current was taking the cutter crabwise towards the brig's counter. Hope must have realized there was no more time left. He said quietly, 'Boat your oars! Stand by, bowman!'

The oars rumbled across the thwarts, but Bolitho knew from experience that the noise which seemed deafening on the cool breeze would be nothing to a man up on the brig's forecastle.

Eden whispered, 'What's Mr T-Tregorren going to do?'

Bolitho could feel his spine chilling under the tension. He heard Hope drawing his sword very carefully from its scabbard, crouching to peer up at the brig's poop as it rose steadily above the boat.

He replied, 'Once we have boarded her, he will attack from the bows, cut the cable and –'

Hope snapped, '*Ready*, lads!'

There was a sudden explosion which seemed to come from far out to sea. A dull red glow spread and glittered on the water, making each part of the swell shine like silk. Another explosion, and still another.

Hope exclaimed, 'Dewar's marines have started already!'

He staggered and all but fell as the cutter ground into the brig's quarter and the bowman hurled his grapnel up and over the rail.

'*At 'em, lads!*' Hope's voice, after the stealth and the suspense, was like a thunderclap. '*Come on!*'

Scrambling and yelling like madmen they swarmed up the side and open gunports in a solid mass of bodies. Someone encountered a loosely rigged boarding net, but even as voices shouted with alarm from below the net was severed, and with Hope and his coxswain in the lead they swept on to the unfamiliar deck.

It was like a scene from an inferno. The British seamen charging across the deck, their faces and wild eyes revealed in the reflected red flashes and the exploding charges at the end of the island.

Two figures ran from the forecastle and a pistol cracked out from a companion-way. A seaman fell sobbing, another jabbed down one of the running figures with his cutlass and hacked him across the neck as he fell for good measure.

More shots now, the balls slamming into the planking or hissing away over the sea. The brig's crew were crowding through the two main hatches, and a ragged volley of pistol and musket fire cut down several of Hope's men.

The lieutenant yelled, 'Bring the swivel from the cutter!'

He caught a man who was hurled aside by a musket ball and lowered him roughly to the deck, adding between gasps, 'Where is that bloody Tregorren?'

The forepart of the brig now seemed full of men, pale and crouching. Darting between familiar objects to take cover and fire on the retreating boarding party.

Hope said desperately, 'If we can't get to grips, we're done for!'

With a pistol in his left hand, his curved hanger in the other, he shouted, 'Close quarters, lads!' Then he charged along the deck and threw himself amongst the nearest marksmen. Shouts of surprise gave way to screams and yells as Hope fired his pistol into a man's chest and slashed another with his hanger. Cursing and cheering the remaining boarders followed him, striking out at anything which moved.

Bolitho fired both of Marrack's pistols into the crowd and thrust them into his belt. He drew his own hanger and parried away a pike which plunged towards him like a spear.

Despite all the danger and terror he found he was able to remember his first boarding attack. A lieutenant had taken away his midshipman's dirk and had said scornfully, 'That's only fit for playing games. You need a man's weapon for this kind of work!' He thought of Grenfell's dirk hanging in the *Gorgon*. He had left his behind, too.

A face loomed above him, the man screaming like

a fiend, although in what language Bolitho could not tell. He felt a violent blow on the side of his head and saw the man's arm going up, his sword pale against the black sky.

Bolitho twisted his body round and struck upwards with the hanger. He felt the pain of the blow lance up his arm, saw the man and sword fall into the gasping, struggling figures as if swallowed up.

He heard a shrill cry and saw Eden groping on the deck, while above him a figure swung a musket like a club.

A pistol exploded, revealing the man's glaring eyes, his fierce concentration giving way to a distorted mask of agony as a pistol ball flung him down.

Bolitho dragged Eden to his feet, hacking out at a running figure, but feeling the blade slice through the air.

Hope shouted, 'Swivel gun!' He gestured to the little rail across the poop. 'Lively there! Fall back!'

They needed no bidding. Parrying and slashing, dragging the wounded as best they could, the survivors fought their way aft to the poop.

Hope bellowed, 'Down, lads!' He thrust at a charging man with his hanger even as the coxswain put a match to the swivel gun which he had mounted on the rail.

The man cut down by Hope's sword must have been carrying a loaded pistol, for as the swivel let out a savage bang and sent a packed charge of canister shot into the advancing shadows the pistol hit the deck and fired even though its owner was dead. The ball struck the lieutenant in the shoulder and he fell beside the smoking swivel without a sound.

As their ears recovered from the swivel's vicious detonation Bolitho heard the cries and screams of men caught in the deadly canister. No wonder old seamen called a swivel 'the daisy-cutter'.

Then from right forward in the beakhead he heard the familiar harsh tones of Lieutenant Tregorren, the sudden rush of feet and the cheers of the other boat's crew.

It was more than enough for the brig's company. Sharks or not, they were leaping overboard, ignoring the yells and curses of their comrades who were too badly hurt to follow.

Tregorren strode aft, pausing merely to bring a belaying pin down on the skull of someone trying to climb on to the main chains.

He peered at the men by the rail. 'Take care of Mr Hope!' The belaying pin pointed and gestured like an obscene fist. 'Two men on the wheel! Mr Dancer, pass the word to cut the cable!' He rocked back on his heels, his eyes searching amongst the rigging. 'Hands aloft and loose tops'ls! Come along, jump about, my children, if you don't want to run ashore!'

Bolitho knelt beside the wounded lieutenant, feeling his pain, his strength ebbing away.

He said, 'That was a brave thing you did, sir.'

Hope said between his teeth, 'Nothing else I could do.' He tried to pat Bolitho's arm. 'You'll know what I mean one day.'

Tregorren towered above them. 'Mr Eden! Take

charge of this officer!' He faced Bolitho. 'So you're still with us, eh?' He shrugged. 'Well, get aloft and chase those laggards!'

The brig was already heeling in the offshore breeze, her hastily released topsails flapping and cracking like musket fire as she tilted free of her severed cable.

'Put up your helm!'

Several shots whimpered overhead, fired by whom, nobody knew.

'Loose the heads'ls!' Tregorren seemed everywhere. 'Lay her on the starboard tack!'

Bolitho clung to the shrouds and stared abeam where a fire was still burning fiercely to show where the marines had created a diversion.

Tiny lanterns moved this way and that, and he realized they were on the other vessel, which had already changed her bearing considerably.

After the long pull around the headland, the apprehension and fear, the actual cutting-out had taken less than twenty minutes. It seemed incredible, and as he paused to think of the nearness of death he felt the sweat like ice-rime on his spine.

He slid down a backstay and found Tregorren bellowing orders down the after companion.

Dancer ran across the deck and said, 'God, I was worried for you! I thought we were never going to engage!'

He turned as a man yelled, 'Sir! There's a whole lot of British seamen battened down 'ere!'

Tregorren snapped, 'See to them! No doubt they are some of the brig's own company.' He caught the man's arm. 'But prisoners, sick or bloody well dying, I want 'em up here on deck!'

He lowered his face to the compass box. 'Hold her steady, quartermaster. As close to the wind as you can. I want no mauling from that battery!'

'Aye, aye, sir.' The men at the wheel eased the spokes deftly. 'Full an' bye, sir! West by south!'

Bolitho watched the figures emerging from the main hatch. Even in the darkness he could sense their disbelief as they were helped and pushed on to the open deck.

One man lurched aft and touched his forehead.

'Starkie, sir. Master's mate of the *Sandpiper*.' He swayed, and would have fallen but for Bolitho.

Tregorren was watching the released seamen, his chin sunk on his neckcloth.

'You the senior?'

'Aye, sir. Cap'n Wade and the other officers were killed.' He dropped his eyes. 'We have been in hell, sir.'

'Possibly.'

Tregorren strode to the foot of the mainmast and squinted up at the flapping topsail.

'Get some of those hands to work and set the spanker and then the fores'l. I want to get some sea-room.'

He turned and added shortly, 'Well, Mr Starkie, you can take charge aft as you are the best qualified.' He looked him slowly up and down, as if his eyes could pierce the darkness. 'Although it would seem you are less so for defending one of His Majesty's ships, eh?'

He hurried away, shouting for Dancer and thrusting through the dazed seamen like a plough.

The master's mate consulted the compass and the set of the topsail and said harshly. 'He had no cause to speak like that. We had no chance.' He looked at Bolitho and added, 'You fought well back there. Some of these devils were laughing at what they would do if your ship tried to force home an attack.'

'But who are they?'

Starkie let out a great sigh. 'Pirates, corsairs, call 'em what you will, but I swear I have seen none worse, and I have been at sea all my years.'

Bolitho saw two men carrying Lieutenant Hope to the companion and prayed he would be strong enough to survive. Several seamen had died, and it was a miracle there were not more to be buried.

Starkie said, 'They kept us aboard to crew the poor *Sandpiper*. Like galley slaves we were. Beaten and treated like scum. They had only enough hands for the guns. But enough to keep us cowed, I can tell you.'

Eden had joined them. 'Any midshipmen, w-were there?'

Starkie looked at him for several seconds. 'Two. Only two. Mr Murray died in the attack. Mr Flowers, he was about your age, well, they killed him later.' He turned away. 'Now leave me be, I don't want to think about it.'

Tregorren came aft again. He sounded almost jovial as he called, 'She answers well, Mr Starkie. A fine little vessel. Fourteen guns too, I see.'

Eden said, 'Mr S-Starkie says that the pirates are the worst he's s-seen, sir!'

Tregorren was still studying the brig, his head cocked as the sails shuddered and banged before the rudder brought the ship back on course again.

'Indeed, indeed. Well, the other pirate vessel has weighed.' He faced Starkie. 'And where would she be going, d'you reckon?'

Starkie shrugged. 'They have another rendezvous to the north of here. Cap'n Wade was searching for it when we were attacked.'

'I see.' Tregorren walked aft to the taffrail. 'Be first light in an hour or so. We will be able to signal *Gorgon*. Put a good man aloft as lookout. We may be able to catch that one and give him a nice dance at the end of a halter.'

He swung angrily on Eden. 'Well, what are *you* gaping at? I hear you were useless during the attack! Weeping for your mother, were you? Nobody to protect you?'

Bolitho said, 'Easy, sir, some of the people are listening.'

'And damn you for your impertinence!' Tregorren's mood had changed like a savage squall. 'I'll have no more of it!'

Bolitho stood his ground. 'Mr Eden was knocked down during the boarding, sir.' He could feel his caution dropping away, his future already in ruins. But he was sick of Tregorren's sarcasm and brutality towards those unable to fight back. 'We were, you recall, outnumbered, sir. We had been expecting some support.'

Tregorren stared at him as if suffering a seizure. 'Are you suggesting –' He tugged at his neckcloth. 'Are you daring to suggest that I was late in boarding?' He leaned forward, his face inches from Bolitho's. '*Well, are you?*'

'I was saying that Mr Eden did well, sir. He had lost his weapon, and he is *twelve years old*, sir.'

They faced each other, oblivious to everything about them.

Then Tregorren nodded very slowly. 'So be it, Mr Bolitho. You will join the masthead lookout until I say differently. When we return to the ship I intend to have you put under arrest for gross insubordination.' He nodded again. 'See how the family likes *that*, eh?'

Bolitho felt his heart pumping against his ribs like a hammer. He had to repeat over and over in his mind: *He wants me to strike him. He wants me to strike him.* It would make Tregorren's actions complete, and for Bolitho final.

'Is that all, sir?' He barely recognized his own voice.

'Aye.' The lieutenant swung away, his sudden move making the mesmerized spectators scatter like rabbits. 'For the present.'

Dancer walked to the main shrouds with him and said hotly, 'That was a foul thing to say! I felt like knocking him to the deck, Dick!'

'So did I.' Bolitho swung himself on to the ratlines and stared up at the mainyard. 'And he knew it.'

Dancer said awkwardly, 'Never mind. We took

the brig. That must count for something with Captain Conway.'

'It is all we have.' He started to climb. 'Be off, Martyn, or he'll have you all aback, too.'

'When you have finished, Mr Dancer!' The voice searched him out from the shadows. 'Be so good as to find a cook and have the galley fire lit. These people look like scarecrows, and I can't abide filth!'

Dancer called, 'At once, sir!'

He looked up at the black shrouds, but Bolitho had already vanished.

7

Mr Starkie's Story

RICHARD BOLITHO clung to a stay and watched the sky brightening reluctantly across the horizon. Little more than a grey blur, but in hours it would be almost too hot to think.

He felt the mast shiver and vibrate as the *Sandpiper* responded eagerly to her bulging sails. He wondered how the wounded were getting on, if Lieutenant Hope was better, or giving way to his injury.

A few figures were just visible on the brig's narrow poop and below the mainmast. He thought he could smell food from the galley and felt his stomach contract painfully. He could not remember when he had last eaten, and found himself hating Tregorren for keeping him aloft without relief.

The lieutenant had been right about one thing. When the news reached the Bolitho home in Falmouth it would have lost the unfairness and hostility of the moment. It would be seen only as Tregorren intended. That Bolitho had acted badly and with insubordination against a superior officer.

He heard heavy breathing and saw Dancer hauling himself up to the crosstrees beside him.

He said, 'You'd better watch out, Martyn!'

Dancer shook his head. 'It's all right, Dick. Mr Starkie sent me. He's worried about our lieutenant.'

Bolitho looked at him. 'Mr Hope? Is he worse?'

'He is as before.' Dancer clutched at a stay as the brig heeled violently in a sudden gust. 'It is Tregorren who is causing the concern.' He grinned. 'Although I must say I can't muster much grief!'

Bolitho reached out and stretched his cramped limbs. He was aching from exposure and felt clammy with salt spray.

Dancer added, 'Mr Starkie thinks that he has a fever.'

They slid down to the deck together and found the master's mate by the wheel with the helmsmen.

Starkie said abruptly, 'It'll be dawn soon. I can't understand it. He's like a man possessed down there. I dunno what we'll do if we run into more trouble.' He looked away, his voice brittle. 'I can't take being a prisoner again. Not after what we've suffered, and that's God's truth!'

Bolitho replied, 'We'll go to him.' He touched Dancer's arm. 'But I'm no surgeon.'

In the tiny cabin where *Sandpiper*'s last captain had enjoyed his privacy and suffered his anxieties, they found Tregorren slumped across a table, his face buried in his arms. The cabin stank of spirits or coarse wine, and as the brig lifted and plunged across the broken water Bolitho heard glass rolling about beneath the cot, and in the glare of a solitary lantern saw that there were many such bottles in a rack against the bulkhead.

Dancer murmured grimly, 'Mr Tregorren has surely found his heaven!'

Bolitho leaned over the table. 'I'll try and rouse him. You keep clear.' He seized the lieutenant's shoulders and heaved him backwards over the chair.

He had been expecting to see a man the worse for drink.

Dancer exclaimed, 'In God's name, Dick, he looks like death!'

Tregorren had a terrible pallor, and more so because his normally ruddy complexion was patchy grey, and when his eyes flickered open very slowly he seemed quite dazed, like someone suffering extreme shock.

He started to speak, but his speech was so thick he had to clear his throat with a series of loud retches.

Bolitho asked, 'Are you ill, sir?' He saw Dancer try to hide a grin and added hastily, 'Mr Starkie was worried for you.'

'Was he?' Tregorren tried to stand but fell back in the chair with a terrible groan. 'Get that bottle!' His fingers were like claws as he seized the bottle and took a long, desperate swallow. 'I don't know what's happening.' He was speaking in a vague, slurred voice. 'Can't control my body.' He retched and tried to rise again. 'Must get to the heads.'

Bolitho and Dancer hauled him to his feet, and for a few moments the three of them swayed and reeled to the motion as if in a weird dance.

Dancer muttered, 'He's done it this time! What our old doctor would call the *bloody flux*! The man is coming apart!'

As they lurched through the bulkhead door Bolitho saw Eden watching from another small cabin where Hope had been since being carried below.

'Give a hand here, Tom! We have to get him to the heads!'

Eden said brightly, 'He l-looks t-terrible, to be sure.'

When they reached the deck the air was like wine after the overpowering stench in the cabin.

Starkie hurried from the wheel. 'Is it fever then?'

Eden piped, 'H-he has the g-gout, Mr Starkie. I have been s-saying s-so all along. He h-has been taking medicine to ease the pain, but I s-suspect has over indulged.'

They all stared at the diminutive midshipman who had suddenly emerged as their only source of medical knowledge.

'Well, what'll we do?' Starkie sounded lost.

Eden regarded the sagging, groaning figure and replied, 'When he g-gets b-back to the ship the s-surgeon will t-take care of him. There's n-nothing we can d-do.' He grimaced. 'S-serve him right.'

'Be that as it may.' Starkie watched Dancer clinging to the lieutenant's coat to stop him from falling clean across the bulwark. 'We're going to need him shortly.'

Dancer stared at him. 'I don't see that. We can signal *Gorgon* and the captain will know what to do.'

Starkie regarded him bleakly. 'You've not noticed. The wind has shifted to the nor'-east. It'd take your ship all day to beat up to this position, that is even if your cap'n knows what's happening.'

Dancer persisted, 'Then what is to stop us from running down on her?'

Starkie said, 'I'm only a master's mate, and one right glad to be safe and free again, but I know the Navy, and I know captains. *Sandpiper* is well placed to head off the enemy, or at least follow her to her hiding place.' He shrugged. 'But without an officer, I'm not so sure. You get no reward for empty heroics, and that's for certain in any navy.'

They looked at Eden as he said in a small voice, 'We're *not* going to the *Gorgon*?'

Bolitho noticed that he had even lost his stammer in his anxiety.

He said quietly, 'Come over here, Tom.' He took the boy's arm and asked calmly, 'What did you do to Mr Tregorren?'

Eden stared at the deck, his hands moving in agitation.

'I knew he was t-trying to t-treat himself by p-putting medicine in his w-wine. I s-saw it on a flask in his c-cabin. *Vin Antim*, like my f-father uses in m-matters of g-gout.' He added wretchedly, 'So I p-put a large m-measure in one of his b-bottles. He must have d-drunk all of it, and a full b-bottle of b-brandy as well.'

Bolitho stared at him. 'You might have killed him!'

'B-but I thought we were rejoining the sh-ship,

you see. I just w-wanted him to s-suffer for all the things he s-said to you, and to m-me.' He shook his head. 'And now you s-say we'll not be joining *Gorgon* r-right away?'

Bolitho breathed out slowly. 'So it seems.'

Dancer steadied the lieutenant as he staggered away from the bulwark. 'Get some men to help this officer to the cabin!'

Bolitho said, 'What now, I wonder?'

As if in answer he heard the lookout yell, 'Deck there! Sail on the lee bow!'

They ran to the nettings but the sea to leeward was still in deep shadow.

Starkie said bitterly, 'So the devil's downwind of us. He stands between us and safety.'

'How well d'you know this coast?' Bolitho's question seemed to come out all on its own.

'Good enough.' Starkie peered at the compass as if to gather his thoughts. 'It's a bad one to try and outpace a frigate.'

Bolitho thought of the *Gorgon* to the south of their position. Maybe the captain did not even know they had cut out the *Sandpiper*, and believed she had fled with the frigate.

Starkie was saying, 'We'd been searching for pirates for months, and Cap'n Wade got some information from a Genoese trader that there was one such vessel in these waters. At the time, the cap'n thought there was only a small ship, and probably not much of a craft at that. But this pirate is no fool, believe me. They say he is half-French and half-English, but one thing is certain, he's thrown in his lot with some Algerine corsairs who have come from the Mediterranean to prey on slavers and honest traders alike.'

Bolitho looked at Dancer and asked softly, 'Are there many of them?'

'Enough. They were short-handed when they took *Sandpiper*, but new men are joining their ranks every day. It doesn't matter what race or country they come from. I'm told that if they swear allegiance to Islam they can be anything they like. The frigate was Spanish before they took her off Oran, and she is commanded by this Jean Gauvin. A madman, if ever I saw one, and without fear. The corsair who forced some Senegalese traders to open the fortress for him is Raïs Haddam. He put our officers to death. Slowly, and in front of our people. It was terrible to see and hear it.'

Nobody spoke, and as Bolitho watched Starkie's tanned features he could see him reliving the horror as if it had just happened.

'We anchored just off the fortress. It was a fine day, and the people were in high spirits. And why not, for we were going home in a month more or so. The frigate lay near us, wearing Spanish colours. The fortress too was flying a trading company flag.' He gave a shudder. 'I suppose Cap'n Wade should have known or suspected. But he was only a lieutenant, no more'n twenty-three. We lowered the boats and went ashore to meet the governor of the island. Instead we were surrounded, and the fortress battery put down a few balls around the *Sandpiper* just to let the watch know they had no chance.'

'After the killing and the torture was over, this Algerine corsair, Raïs Haddam, spoke to the rest of us. Told us that if we worked the ship for him we might be spared.' He looked away. 'Gauvin was there too, and when one of the midshipmen tried to protest it was Gauvin who ordered him to be killed. They burned him alive on the foreshore!'

Dancer whispered, 'My God!'

'Aye.' Starkie stared past him into the shadows. 'Haddam has gathered the scum of the earth to his banner.'

Bolitho nodded. 'Raïs Haddam. I have heard my father and his friends speak of him. He has raided the Algerian coast for years, and is now looking elsewhere for his corsairs.' He glanced at the paling sky. 'I never expected to meet up with him!'

Starkie said bitterly, 'There is no time left to prepare a defence.'

Bolitho looked at their faces, sensing despair and defeat. Dancer was too new to the Navy to know anything different. Starkie was still too stunned by his captivity to offer advice.

Bolitho said quietly, 'Then we must prepare an attack.'

He thought of Tregorren, filled with pain and drink because of Eden's ruse. Of Hope, barely breathing, a musket ball in his shoulder. Of their seamen, some bewildered at their sudden releases and others quite exhausted from the savage fighting on this same deck.

Starkie exclaimed, 'Gauvin's ship mounts twenty-four guns to our fourteen little squeakers!'

Dancer asked, 'When *Sandpiper* was used to seize the barquentine, what happened to her crew?'

'Over the side.' Starkie looked grim-faced. 'Gutted like pigs.'

Bolitho said, 'So much for the bad side. Now, what can we do against Gauvin?'

He walked to the weather side, feeling the spray pattering across his face and hands.

'He'll know that *Gorgon* is to the south'rd.' Dancer had joined him. 'And will expect us to try and rejoin her.'

Bolitho glanced at Starkie, wondering if his memory could be trusted.

'If we come about, Mr Starkie, how close could we weather the headland?'

Starkie's eyes widened with alarm. 'Back to that damned island, y'mean?'

'*Towards* it. There is a difference.'

'It's dangerous. You should know that, if you rounded the headland under oars. There are reefs a'plenty, many not even marked on the charts.'

Bolitho said half to himself, 'Off Cornwall there are some islands called the Scillies. A Bristol trader was being chased by a French privateer in the last war. The trader's master had no chance of outpacing the enemy, but he knew his islands well. He sailed right across one reef and the Frenchie followed him. Ripped out his keel. There were none saved.'

Starkie stared at him with amazement. 'You want to steer a course through the reef? Is that what you're asking me to do?'

A weak ray of sunlight lanced across the upper

rigging and made the topgallant yard glitter like a crucifix.

'Do we have a choice?' Bolitho watched him gravely. 'Captivity, and possibly death to make another example, *or* . . .' The word hung in the air.

Starkie nodded firmly. 'We'll probably die anyway, but God, it's a chance I'd rather take.' He rubbed his rough hands together. 'I suggest we call the hands and shorten sail to come about. If the wind goes against us we'll end up on a lee shore.' He chuckled suddenly, dropping the years from his lined face. 'By God, Mr, whatever your name is, I'd hate to serve under you when you're a cap'n. My nerves would give out afore long!'

Bolitho smiled sadly as more light opened up the deck to display the dull stains where men had fought and died, the jagged splinters left by the swivel gun.

He looked at Eden. 'See how Mr Hope is. Try and get him to take some brandy.' He saw the boy flinch. '*Not* Mr Tregorren's bottle, if you please.'

As Eden started for the companion he added, 'And try to find a flag. I want this pirate to recognize *Sandpiper* under her rightful colours today.'

Dancer watched him in silence. Then he said to Starkie, 'I have never seen such a mood in him. He means to fight. It's no deception.'

The master's mate walked to the lee rail and spat on to the creaming wash.

'Well, m'lad, when Gauvin sees the flag, that'll do it right enough. It's not a sight he's very fond of.'

Eden reappeared carrying a roll of bunting.

'Found one, Dick. Hidden under the b-brandy b-bottles in the cabin.'

'How are the lieutenants?' Starkie spoke sharply, perhaps still hoping that someone else would appear to take over responsibility.

Eden pouted. 'M-Mr Hope is breathing a l-little better. Mr Tregorren is in a filthy s-state.'

Starkie sighed. 'Very well. Pipe the hands to the braces. No point in delaying things any more.'

Bolitho gripped the poop rail and watched the seamen hurrying to braces and halliards, their movements jerky, as if they were still shocked and uncertain.

It was like a dream. Of pirates, and brave young men fighting their country's enemies.

But it was fast becoming a nightmare. Only the first part was right, he thought. A little brig, a demoralized company, and some boys to lead them.

He thought of his father, and of Captain Conway, grave-faced and confident behind their guns and their seamanship.

He said, 'Run up the colours, Mr Eden.' Even the formality surprised him. 'Then stand by to come about.'

8

Across the Reef

'Sou'-sou'-east, sir! Full an' bye!'

Bolitho gripped the hammock nettings and watched the *Sandpiper* dip her lee bulwark steeply towards the sea. Spray and drifting foam dashed across the deck, and when he glanced up at the main yard he saw it was bending like a huge bow as the seamen worked to set more sail.

Starkie remarked hoarsely, 'The wind's freshening a bit.' He shaded his eyes to peer at the masthead pendant. 'But it's holding steady from the nor'-east.' He added grimly, 'So far.'

Bolitho hardly heard him. He was watching the brig's efforts as she lifted and smashed down on to each successive line of whitecaps.

From the moment they had brought the ship about and turned her gilded figurehead towards the land again he had sensed the change around him. Even the *Sandpiper*'s original hands, many showing festering cuts and cruel injuries from their captivity, were shouting to each other, doing all they could to set every stitch of canvas short of tearing the masts out of her. Only when they looked aft did they falter. Perhaps, Bolitho thought, they still expected to see their young captain at the rail, as if by hoping they could hold their memories at bay.

Dancer shouted above the din of canvas and wind, 'She's flying, Dick!'

He nodded, seeing the bows dip into a steep-sided roller and hurl the spray high over the beakhead in a solid white sheet.

'Aye.' He looked across the quarter. 'Can you see the frigate?' He gripped Dancer's arm. 'There she is! And she's making more sail.'

As the gloom of the night retreated slowly towards the open sea he saw the topsails and topgallants of the other ship, changing shape as she too changed tack and came end-on in pursuit. He pointed to the flag above his head, making a bright patch against the washed-out sky.

'Mr Starkie was right, it seems. Our enemy is roused!'

Starkie walked up to the weather side, his body leaning against the deck's steep angle.

'I'm holding her as close to the wind as I dare. Bring her up another point and she'll not answer.'

Bolitho took a glass from a rack by the compass box and trained it towards the land. As he steadied it through the maze of shrouds and vibrating halliards he saw the faces of some of the seamen loom towards him, and wondered what they were thinking as the brig headed for the shore, to the place where their pain and humiliation had begun.

Then he saw the headland, jutting out in a welter of breakers like the prow of a Roman galley.

How different it had looked from the cutter, all that while ago. He had to shake himself to realize it was only yesterday.

The sea looked rougher, and driven by the gusty wind was surging amongst a necklace of rocks as if to beckon them all to destruction.

There was a dull bang, and when he swung aft towards the frigate he saw a smear of smoke moving rapidly with the wind.

Starkie said, 'Just a sighting shot. She's too lively to hit us at this range.'

Bolitho did not reply. He was watching the frigate's great foresail writhing and puffing in disorder as her captain brought her up into the wind. She was almost in irons when the foresail filled and hardened again, the lee gunports heeling down until they were awash.

Dancer said, 'She's worked across our stern, Dick.'

'Yes. She intends to take the wind gage from us.' He still kept his eyes on the frigate until they watered painfully. 'But it means she will stand the closer inshore when we pass the headland.'

Dancer stared at him. 'Can we really get through?'

Starkie heard him and called, 'You'll be asking if we can walk on water next!' He seized the wheel and added his own strength to the helmsmen's. 'Watch your head, damn you!'

Another bang. This time Bolitho saw the white feathers of spray kicking across each line of waves as the ball skipped past their stern.

He looked at the *Sandpiper*'s six-pounders. Very suitable for hit-and-run attacks on enemy merchant-men, or for running down pirates and smugglers.

For taking on a frigate they were useless.

'Send another good lookout aloft, Martyn.' He staggered as the deck shook violently in a sudden trough. 'The *Gorgon* may be in sight.'

But there was no sign of the big seventy-four. Just the pursuing frigate, and the first view of the island on the far side of the bay.

As before, it looked pale and strangely tranquil in the early sunlight, and it was hard to accept all that had happened there.

Starkie had said earlier that the island was even now packed with wretched slaves, men and young girls who had been gathered by the traders from all parts of Africa.

And before long many of them would be sailing west to the Americas and the Indies. If they were lucky they might end their days in comfortable captivity, rather like dependent servants. Those less fortunate would eke out their lives like animals. When their usefulness was over, their strength used up, they would be discarded.

Bolitho had heard it said that slave ships, like the oared galleys of Spain, could be traced at sea by their terrible smell. The stench of bodies crammed together, unable to move, incapable of making even the simplest comfort for themselves.

Bang. A ball hissed overhead and slapped through the foretopsail like an iron fist.

'Closer.' Starkie had his thumbs in his belt, his eyes

fixed on the frigate. 'He's overhauling us more quickly now.'

'Deck there! Breakers on the lee bow!'

Starkie ran to the rail and snatched a glass. 'Aye, that's 'em. The first line of reefs.' He glared aft at the helmsmen. 'Let her fall off a point!'

The wheel creaked, and brought a protest of flapping canvas from the topgallants.

'Sou' by east, sir!'

'Steady as you go!'

Bolitho could tell from the worsening motion, the way every spar and sail seemed to be quivering in protest, that they were entering shallower water and crossing a fierce undertow.

Starkie said, 'Better shorten sail.'

Bolitho looked at him, his voice almost pleading. 'If we do, he'll take us before *he's* in any danger.'

The master's mate eyed him impassively. 'As you say.'

Eden scrambled through the canting companion, his eyes frightened as he peered astern for the enemy.

'Mr Hope is c-calling for y-you, Dick.'

He ducked as the frigate's bow-chaser hurled a shot close abeam, throwing a waterspout high into the air like a surfacing whale.

Bolitho nodded. 'I'll go to him. Call me if anything happens.'

Starkie was peering through his telescope at the nearest line of breakers. By allowing his ship to fall downwind just a trifle he had brought the bowsprit and tapering jib boom almost in line with the tell-tale surf.

He said over his shoulder, 'Don't worry. You'll *know*.'

Bolitho groped his way from the companion ladder and entered the small, hutch-like cabin.

Hope was sprawling in a cot, his eyes very bright as Bolitho bent over him.

'I've heard that the fourth lieutenant is unwell?' His face was ashen. 'Damn him, why did he hold off his attack?' He was rambling vaguely. 'My shoulder. Oh God, they'll lop off my arm when we get to the ship.'

The pain and the despair seemed to steady him. 'Are you managing?'

Bolitho forced a smile. 'We have a good master's mate on deck, sir. Mr Dancer and I are trying to look like veterans.'

Another dull bang penetrated the humid cabin, and Bolitho felt the hull tremble as a ball slammed down hard alongside. Too close.

Hope gasped, 'You cannot fight a frigate!'

'Would you have me strike, sir?'

'*No!*' He shut his eyes and groaned with pain. 'I don't know. I only understand that I should be helping you. Doing something. Instead . . .'

Bolitho watched his desperation with new understanding. Hope, the fifth lieutenant, had been closer to him than the other officers. He always pretended not to show his concern for the midshipmen under his charge, displayed an outer skin of hardness which had been taken as brutal on some occasions. But his constant presence amongst them had proved that some of his unsympathetic criticism had been both necessary and beneficial. As he had remarked more than once: *This ship needs officers not children.*

And now he was lying there, broken and helpless.

Bolitho said quietly, 'I will come for advice whenever I can, sir.'

One hand moved out of the bloodstained cot and gripped his.

'Thank you.' Hope was barely able to focus his eyes. 'God be with you!'

'Below there!' It was Dancer's voice. 'The frigate's running out her starboard guns!'

'I'm coming!'

Bolitho ran for the ladder. Thinking of Hope, of all of them.

In the short time he had been below the sunlight had broken from the land and changed the sea into an endless array of leaping wavecrests.

Starkie shouted, 'Wind's backed a piece! Nothing much. But the frigate's going to make a run for us, I reckon!'

Bolitho took a glass from a seaman and trained it over the nettings. The frigate was barely a mile off the larboard quarter, sails braced hard round to hold the wind, her starboard guns showing above the churning wash along her side like black teeth.

He saw her outline alter slightly as she came up a point or so to windward, the sunlight lancing on weapons and telescopes, and on the large black flag at her mainmast truck. He could even distinguish her name painted on weatherworn scrollwork beneath her beakhead. *Pegaso.* Probably the original name she had carried under the Spanish flag.

'She's fired!'

A stabbing line of orange tongues belched from her gunports, the untimed broadside whipping past *Sandpiper*'s stern and a few moaning above the poop.

Bolitho said, 'Alter course, Mr Starkie. Two points to windward, if you can.'

Starkie opened his mouth to protest and changed his mind. He watched some barely concealed rocks dashing past the starboard side. Well clear, but it meant they were committed. Amongst the sprawling reefs like a fly in a web.

'Man the braces there! Let go and haul!' Dancer hurried to lend a hand. '*Heave*, lads!'

Above the plunging hull every shroud and sail seemed to be booming and creaking in disorder as the bows crept round and then steadied on the next spit of land.

Another ragged broadside, the balls skipping harmlessly astern and bringing a feeble cheer from a watching seaman who did not realize the peril he was in.

Bolitho shouted, 'Get the best gun captain, Martyn! Lively!'

'Sou'-east by south, sir!' The helmsman sounded dazed.

'Very well.'

Starkie turned momentarily to watch as a grizzled old seaman in patched trousers and a check shirt ran aft and knuckled his forehead.

'Taylor, zur.'

'Well, Taylor, I want you to pick your two most

reliable crews and man the aftermost six-pounders, starboard side.'

Taylor blinked at the midshipman, probably thinking Bolitho was at last going mad. The enemy, after all, was on the opposite side.

Bolitho was speaking quickly, his mind blank to everything but the frigate and *Sandpiper*'s bearing from her. He tried to remember everything he had learned or had had beaten into him from the age of twelve until this day. 'Double-shotted. I know it's a risk. But I want you to hit the frigate's bows when I give the word.'

Taylor nodded slowly. 'Aye, zur.' He gestured with a tarred thumb. 'I fathom yer meanin', zur.' He ambled away, bawling out names and examining two six-pounders by the poop as he did so.

Bolitho looked at Starkie, his eyes level. 'I want to wear ship and pass out through the reef again. The frigate's bound to follow. He will have all the advantage with the wind under his coat-tails.' He saw Starkie nodding grimly. 'For just a few moments we will have him under our guns.' He smiled, the effort freezing his lips. 'Such as they are. He'll not be expecting us to turn and fight. Not now.'

Starkie stared beyond the bows like a man seeking a way out.

'I think I know a passage. It's not much.' He made a sweeping movement with his fist. 'I'm not sure about the depth. A few fathoms, no more, if I'm any judge.'

Thuds and bangs told Bolitho that Taylor and his men were almost ready.

A sudden roar of cannon fire made him realize that the frigate was still determined to cripple *Sandpiper* and then bring her to close action.

Aloud he murmured, 'Not this time, my friend.'

Starkie lowered his telescope as the frigate's iron shrieked overhead and brought down several lengths of broken rigging and a few blocks. The hull gave a violent jerk, and Bolitho knew they had taken their first direct hit.

He looked at Starkie as the latter called, 'Ready when you are.' He wiped his forehead with his wrist. He was streaming with sweat.

'Man the braces! Stand by to wear ship!' Bolitho nodded to the two gun crews. '*Run out!*'

He gripped his hands behind him until the force of his hold steadied him. He knew Dancer was staring, as were several of the men at the braces and halliards. Perhaps they were trying to see their own fate in his face.

He heard the old gun captain say, 'Don't yew forget, lads. As we goes about we'll be to lee'rd of that bugger. But it'll give your guns a better chance as we 'eels over like.'

There was a brief lull in the wind, so that just for an instant the sounds of sea and canvas faded. Through his racing thoughts Bolitho heard another sound, that of Tregorren groaning like a bull in agony.

The madness of it, the very hopelessness of their position made the lieutenant's discomfort all the more unreal.

He shook himself back to the present

'Put up your helm! Wear ship!'

Leaning drunkenly with the wind, her beakhead lifting and smashing down in a welter of criss-crossing waves, *Sandpiper* began to respond to canvas and rudder.

The noise was indescribable, so that when the *Pegaso* fired a solitary shot from a bow-chaser the sound was almost lost in the thundering boom of sails, the protest of blocks and bar-taut rigging.

Bolitho saw that the men at the weather braces were hauling with such effort that their bodies were angled back almost to the deck itself. Others ran to aid their companions at halliards and aloft on the yards as they creaked round still further, the sails hardening and swelling like armour to the wind's thrust.

Bolitho tried not to look for the reefs, or at Starkie who had climbed into the shrouds to gauge better their progress towards the breaking surf.

Weakened by the *Pegaso*'s haphazard shots through the upper rigging, more pieces of severed hemp fell unheeded to the deck and across the rigid shoulders of Taylor, the old gun captain.

Round and still further round, the masts and yards creaking violently as the brig wheeled on to the opposite tack, the sea sluicing up and over the lee bulwark, which minutes earlier had been towards the enemy.

Bang. A ball sliced across the heaving water and slammed savagely into the hull, making several men cry out with alarm.

'Get some hands on the pumps!' Bolitho heard himself yelling orders, but felt like an onlooker, detached from all that was happening.

Ice-cold, he watched the enemy swinging around and across the stern, or so it appeared from *Sandpiper*'s violent alteration of course.

'*Now.*' His voice was lost in the din, and he shouted with sudden urgency, 'As you bear! *Fire!*'

He had seen the *Pegaso*'s big foresail starting to angle round as her captain decided to change tack and follow the brig.

He knew Taylor was crouching behind one of the guns, but could not look at him. He heard the hiss of his slow-match, and started with shock as the gun banged out across the water. He saw the *Pegaso*'s foresail pucker and a large hole appear as if by magic. Explored and strained by the wind and by the sudden alteration of course, the hole spread out in every direction, ripping the sail to fragments.

Starkie yelled, 'He's still coming round, sir!'

A lookout's voice cut across Bolitho's thoughts like a saw. 'Breakers to larboard, sir!'

But all he could think of was failure. The double-shotted gun had destroyed a sail, but under full canvas it could make no difference now.

Once through the reef, and it was strange that he had no doubts now Starkie could do it, the pirate would overhaul and board them.

Taylor loped to the second gun, his face creased in concentration. Fierce gestures with his tarred thumb got a handspike moving here, a tug on a gun tackle there.

He crouched down, his eyes like slits as he wheezed, '*Easy* now! Come on, my little one!'

The match went home, and with a grating crash the gun hurled itself inboard, smoke eddying back through the port like choking fog.

Bolitho watched, mesmerized. It took an age, in fact, only seconds. And then as the carefully aimed shot lifted and dropped across the frigate's bows he saw the bulging jib and staysail tear from top to bottom like old rags.

The effect was instantaneous. Caught in the middle of changing tack, her sails already in confusion, the *Pegaso* wallowed heavily in a deep trough, her gunports buried in the sea as she continued to answer the rudder.

Bolitho heard shouts from the lee side and ran to the nettings, his throat like dust as he saw a green-shouldered rock scudding past the *Sandpiper*'s side, barely yards clear. In those split seconds he saw the worn shape of the rock, and some tiny black fish which had managed to remain motionless, despite the wind and current, sheltering behind the reef which could tear out a ship's keel like the string from an orange.

He darted a glance at Dancer. He looked very pale and wild-eyed, his face and chest soaked with spray as he leaned out to watch the enemy's progress.

The *Pegaso* seemed to stagger, as if taken by an opposite squall, then as she tilted upright her main topgallant mast cracked over and fell straight down to the deck, a tangle of rigging and canvas trailing between the shrouds like weed.

Starkie yelled incredulously, 'See that? She hit a reef!' He was croaking with excitement and awe. '*She struck*, by God!'

Bolitho could not tear his eyes away. The frigate must have smashed hard against a rock shoulder even as she lost power from her forward sails in the middle of a tack. Just a few yards had made all the difference, and he could picture the confusion on deck, the rush of men below to seek out the extent of the damage.

It had been enough to bring down a topgallant mast, and she must be leaking badly, he thought. And yet the frigate was still coming on, and as he watched, his eyes aching in the glare, he saw a bow-chaser shoot out an orange tongue, and felt the ball shriek past him and crash into the forecastle like a giant's axe.

Broken rigging and whirling splinters were hurled everywhere, and he saw three seamen smashed against the bulwark, their cries lost in the wind, but their convulsions marked by spreading patterns of blood.

Another ball ripped against the hull and ricocheted away over the sea, the deck bucking as if trying to throw the seamen from their feet.

Bolitho yelled, 'Attend the wounded! Tell Mr Eden to put them below!'

He thought suddenly of Eden's father in his little surgery, attending to people with gout and stomach trouble. What would he think if he could see his twelve-year-old son trying to drag a gasping seaman

to the companion hatch, every foot of the way marked
in pain and blood.

Dancer said despairingly, 'The frigate's closing to
board us!' He did not even flinch as a ball whipped
above the poop, leaving another hole in the pock-
marked sails. 'After all we did!'

Bolitho looked at him and those nearby. The
fight, the pathetic determination were going rapidly.
And who could blame them? The *Pegaso* had matched
their every move, in spite of being surprised. She
was through the reef, and he could see the glitter of
waving cutlasses as some of the men ran from the
guns in readiness to board. He recalled Starkie's
description of what had happened to *Sandpiper*'s
officers, the torture and the final agony of their
deaths.

He drew his hanger and yelled, 'Stand to! Starboard side!' He saw them turn to stare at him
incredulously, their eyes dull with despair.

Bolitho jumped to the weather shrouds and waved
his hanger at the *Pegaso*.

'They'll not take us without a fight!'

Little cameos stood out from the main picture. A
man taking out a knife and honing it back and forth
across his hand, his eyes on the frigate. Another
crossing the deck to face a man who was probably his
best, his only friend. Nothing said. Just an expression
which told far more than words. Eden by the companion hatch, his face like chalk, and a man's blood
already drying on his shirt, like his own would soon
do. Dancer. His hair golden in the sunlight, his chin
lifted as he picked up a cutlass and leaned on it.

Bolitho saw his other hand gripping into his breeches, like a claw, pinching the flesh to shock him from his fear.

A man, wounded in the attack on the brig, was propped against a six-pounder, his legs in bandages, but his fingers busy as he loaded pistols and passed them to the others.

Something like a baying howl came from the *Pegaso*'s crowded deck as she edged closer abeam, the shadows of her masts and yards reaching across the water as if to snare the brig and engulf her.

Bolitho blinked and dashed the sweat from his eyes as he stared at one of the frigate's open gunports. A man, then another, was clambering out and around the black muzzles, and from other ports he saw figures emerging like rats from a sewer.

Starkie exclaimed, 'They're trying to abandon, sir!' He seized his arm and propelled him to the nettings. 'Will you *look* at that!'

Bolitho stood at his side and said nothing. More and more men were leaping from the gunports and being carried away like shavings on a mill-race.

Gauvin, the *Pegaso*'s fanatical captain, must have put guards on every hatch, and as his ship charged in hopeless, maddened pursuit, he would have known that the hull damage was fatal.

Starkie watched the frigate's bow wave falling away as the great weight of inrushing water slowed her down, the sudden pandemonium on the upper deck as everyone at last realized what was happening.

He said harshly, 'Here, put on your coat.' He even

helped Bolitho into it and tugged the collar with its white patches into position.

He pointed to the *Pegaso*, which was starting to head away, the inrush of water playing havoc with the rudder's puny efforts.

'I want him to see you, and I pray to God he'll suffer for what he did.'

When Bolitho looked at him, he added, 'I want him to know he was beaten by a midshipman! A *boy*!'

Bolitho turned away, his ears filled with the sounds of a ship destroying itself, as under full sail she continued to slew round across the glittering crests. He heard guns coming loose from tackles and smashing into the opposite side, and spars falling, trapping the stampeding men under masses of black rigging and canvas.

He heard himself say, 'Shorten sail, Martyn. Call all hands.'

He felt men touching his shoulders, others ran towards him grinning and waving. Not a few were weeping.

'Deck there!' Everyone had forgotten the lonely man at the masthead. 'Sail on th' starboard bow, sir!' The merest pause and then, ''Tis th' *Gorgon*!'

Bolitho waved his hand to the masthead and turned to watch the pirate frigate heeling over, the sea around her filled with flotsam and thrashing, bobbing heads.

Out of the sun's path, across the heaving swell, he also saw a sudden flicker of movement, the knife-edged fins of sharks closing in around the sinking ship. It was over a mile to the nearest beach. It was doubtful if anyone would reach it.

He raised a telescope to look for the *Gorgon*, his eyes misty as he saw her fat black and buff hull, her towering pyramid of canvas rounding the next headland.

In another second he thought he would break, be unable to hide his emotion from those about him.

A great voice bellowed, 'What the *hell* is going on?'

Lieutenant Tregorren was standing half through the companion hatch, and with his blotchy grey face, his hair matted with wine and worse, he looked for all the world like a corpse emerging from a tomb.

Bolitho felt the relief flooding through him like madness. He wanted to laugh and cry all at once, and Tregorren's wild appearance, the realization that he had been completely helpless throughout the fight, broke down all reserves.

He replied in a shaking voice, 'I am sorry we disturbed you, sir.'

Tregorren faced him and tried to focus a pair of angry red eyes.

'*Disturb?*'

'Aye, sir. But we have been fighting a battle.'

Starkie said calmly, 'Fetch Mr Eden. I fear the lieutenant is going to be ill again!'

9

Without Honour

CAPTAIN BEVES CONWAY stood by an open stern window and held one hand to his eyes to protect them from the fierce, reflected glare. Through the windows of his cabin the recaptured brig rolled untidily in the swell, her tan sails barely moving as she idled above her own reflection.

Within a few hours of *Sandpiper*'s hazardous dash through the reef and the complete destruction of the frigate, the wind had dropped to a mere breath, leaving the heavy *Gorgon* and her small consort almost becalmed.

Like a pale yellow smear along the horizon, twisting and wavering in heat-haze, the shore was still visible, but could have been any-where.

Conway turned slowly and studied the group by the bulkhead.

Tregorren, massive and red-eyed, his body swaying to the heavy motion, his face still the colour of ashes.

The three midshipmen, and the master's mate, Mr Starkie, standing slighly apart.

Verling, the first lieutenant, was also present, his nose disapproving as the captain's servant filled glasses of madeira for the crumpled and dishevelled visitors.

The captain took a beautifully cut glass from a tray and held it to the filtered sunlight.

'Your health, gentlemen.' He regarded each of them in turn. 'I do not have to say how gratified I am that *Sandpiper* is again with the fleet.' He turned to listen to the distant tap of hammers across the water as work continued to put right the damage from *Pegaso*'s cannon fire. 'Eventually I will be sending her to report to the admiral at Gibraltar with my despatches.' His gaze rested momentarily on Tregorren. 'To cut out a vessel at anchor is never easy. To do it, and to find the extra agility and skill to run an enemy frigate to ground, is worthy of their lordships' attention.'

Tregorren stared at some point above the captain's shoulder.

'Thank you, sir.'

The captain's eyes moved to the midshipmen. 'To have survived all this will give you scope for putting the experience to work, both for your own advancement and for the Navy in general.'

Bolitho darted a quick glance at Tregorren. The man was still staring at the deckhead, and he looked close to another violent attack of vomiting.

The captain said in the same matter-of-fact tone, 'At first light, while you were entering the reefs, I was searching to the south'rd. Quite by chance we came on a heavy dhow, loaded to the gunwales with black ivory.'

Starkie exclaimed, 'Slaves, sir?'

The captain regarded him coldly. '*Slaves.*' He gestured with his glass. 'I put a boarding party into the vessel, and she is now anchored around the next headland.' He gave a thin smile. 'The slaves I put ashore, although I know not if I have done them a favour.' The smile vanished.

'We have wasted too much time, and lost too many good men. It would take an army to lay siege to the island, and even then it is doubtful how the attack would go.'

He paused as the marine sentry beyond the door shouted, 'Surgeon, sir!'

The servant hurried to open the door as Laidlaw entered, wiping his hands carefully on a scrap of cloth.

'Yes?' The captain sounded sharp.

'You wished to know, sir. Mr Hope is sleeping. I took out the ball, and although I doubt if he'll ever be rid of discomfort, he'll not lose an arm.'

Bolitho looked at Dancer and Eden and smiled. It was something. The rest was over, part of a nightmare which even Tregorren's failure to admit that he had had no hand in the final action could not spoil.

He glanced at Starkie, who was studying Tregorren with something like hatred.

The captain added, 'At dusk, provided the wind returns, which Mr Turnbull *assures* me will, we will make contact with our new prize. At dawn I intend to send *Sandpiper* to chase the dhow towards the fortress. *Gorgon* will, of course, supply full support.'

Bolitho swallowed another glass of madeira, barely realizing that the cabin servant had refilled it more than once. His stomach was quite empty, and the wine was making him feel light-headed and dizzy.

One fact stood out. The captain had no intention of giving in to the pirates who occupied the island. By retaking *Sandpiper* they had added another arm to their reach, and the watchers on the fortress's battery would have been able to see quite clearly how the brig had lured their one major vessel on to the reefs.

Verling snapped, 'Understood?'

Bolitho exclaimed, 'They'll think we're chasing a cargo of slaves, and be too busy firing at *Sandpiper* to watch the dhow, sir?'

The captain looked at him and then glanced across at Tregorren.

'What d'*you* think, Mr Tregorren?'

The lieutenant seemed to come out of a trance. 'Yes, sir. That is . . .'

The captain nodded. 'Quite.'

He walked aft again and studied the brig for some time.

'Mr Starkie will return to his ship and be prepared to assist whichever officers I appoint to take charge, and to sail eventually with my despatches.' He swung round, his eyes hard in the light. 'Had I thought that you had any part in losing *Sandpiper* in the first place, by negligence or lack of courage, I can assure you that you would not be here now, and your chances of advancement would have been smashed.' He smiled, the effort making him older rather than the opposite. 'You did very well, Mr Starkie. I only wish I could keep you in my command. But I think that when you reach higher authority your efforts will be better rewarded.' He nodded. 'Carry on, gentlemen.'

They left the cabin in a daze, the captain already in conference with Verling and the surgeon.

Bolitho shook Starkie's rough hand and exclaimed, 'I'm glad for you! But for your skill, and accepting an idea which to most people would have seemed quite mad, we would not be here at all!'

Starkie studied him gravely, as if searching for something he could not understand.

'But for *you*, I'd still be in irons and awaiting death.'

He turned as Tregorren strode to the companion ladder on his way down to the wardroom.

'I wanted to speak out.' Starkie's eyes were bitter. 'But as you said nothing, I thought it best to hold my peace. He is without honour!'

Eden stammered, 'It's n-not r-right, D-Dick! H-he'll get the c-credit!' He was almost weeping. 'He j-just stood th-there and t-took it all!'

Dancer smiled. 'I think the captain knows more than he's prepared to admit. I watched him. He is balancing the value of the victory against damaging it with envy and shame.' He grinned at Eden. '*And* midshipmen who go round trying to poison their betters!'

Bolitho nodded. 'I agree. Now let us go and eat. Anything, even a ship's rat, will do for me.'

They turned towards the companion ladder and froze.

A figure in an ill-fitting uniform, that of a lieutenant, blocked their way.

He said, 'Nothing to do, eh? Midshipmen are not what they were in my day!'

They crowded round him, and Bolitho said, 'John Grenfell! We thought you dead!'

Grenfell gripped his hand, his face very grim. 'When *City of Athens* was destroyed, some of us managed to find safety on drifting spars. We hauled them together like a little raft, not knowing what was happening.' He dropped his gaze. 'Most of our people were killed. The lucky ones in the cannon fire, the rest when the sharks tore amongst us. The third lieutenant, oh, so many old faces, were slashed to fragments before our eyes.' He shrugged, as if to free himself of the memory. 'But we drifted ashore, and as we made our way along the coast, there, as large as life, was the ship standing in to the beach, and Dewar's bullocks with a dhow full of screaming slaves, an Arab crew and two Portuguese merchants who were so terrified that I think they believed their end had come.' He plucked at his borrowed coat. 'So I have been made acting sixth lieutenant. It will do no harm when my examination is called.' He looked into the distance. 'But I got the chance at a price I would dearly repay if it were possible.'

Bolitho said quietly, 'But *you* are safe.'

Starkie yawned. 'I could sleep for a year.' He grinned at Grenfell. '*Sir*.'

Grenfell walked with them to the ladder. 'I suggest you all get some rest. I have a feeling it will be all the hotter tomorrow, in more ways than one!'

Mr Turnbull's knowledge of weather did not desert him. By the time the first dog watch had run its course both vessels were under way again, their sails filling to the breeze. An hour later the wind had steadied to a fresh northerly, and when the hands were assembled aft the air was like a tonic after the sweaty furnace between decks.

The lieutenants and marine officers were by the poop ladder, watching the captain, who was conferring with Verling and the sailing master.

Petty officers moved amongst the assembled seamen, checking their muster lists and calling out names, while from the lower gundeck Bolitho could hear the screech of a grindstone as the gunner's mates attended to the sharpening of cutlasses and boarding axes. The very sound made him shiver, as it always had.

A lookout bawled, 'Deck there! Vessel at anchor off the larboard bow!'

Dancer had been peering across at *Sandpiper*'s sails. They were creamy in the fading light, and there was nothing visible of the shot holes and patches.

Dallas, the second lieutenant, had taken charge of her for the attack. A man Bolitho knew nothing of, and had barely heard utter more than a few necessary orders since he had joined the ship. But the captain's choice showed that he trusted Dallas for the task. It also suggested he was not entirely satisfied with Tregorren's part in the cutting-out.

When Bolitho had seen Starkie over the side to be taken back to the brig, the master's mate had stared aft towards the captain's slowly pacing figure. He had grinned.

'It's how you gets to *be* a post-captain, young feller, knowing them things!'

'All midshipmen lay aft to the quarterdeck!'

They hurried along the gangway and found Verling waiting by the lee nettings, one foot tapping with impatience.

'Three of you will be required for the attack.' He scowled as Marrack made to speak. 'Not you. You will be needed for the signal party.' His cold eyes rested on Bolitho. 'As you have just returned to your proper duties with us, I cannot order you to take part either. Mr Pearce,' he turned to the sulky looking midshipman from the lower gundeck, 'and . . .'

Bolitho glanced at Dancer who gave the briefest nod.

He called, 'Mr Dancer and I would like to volunteer, sir. We sailed very close to the island. It might be of some use.'

Verling smiled wryly. 'Now that Mr Grenfell has placed his foot on the bottom rung of promotion, you three, apart from Mr Marrack, are the oldest. So I suppose I'd better allow you to go.'

Eden stepped smartly from the rank of midshipmen.

'S-sir! I'd l-like to v-volunteer, too!'

Verling glared down at him. 'Don't you stutter at me, you urchin! Get back in line and hold your noise!'

Eden retreated, beaten before he had started.

Verling nodded, apparently satisfied.

'Boats will be lowered as soon as we heave-to. All the marines and sixty seamen will transfer to that floating hell yonder.'

Dancer whispered, 'The captain is sending everyone he can spare.'

Verling rasped, 'After the raid, should you be spared, Mr Dancer, you will be awarded five days extra duty. *Be silent!*'

The captain walked aft towards the poop, as if on a stroll ashore.

He paused and asked evenly, 'All well, Mr Verling?'

'Aye, sir.'

The captain glanced at the three midshipmen who stood where they had been called.

'Be vigilant.' He looked at his first lieutenant. 'Mr Verling will command the attack, so he will expect your best support, as will I.' He leaned forward, seeking out Eden's small shape. 'You, er, Mr er, will probably be useful assisting the surgeon in your new and er, surprising capacity.'

Neither he nor Verling gave even the hint of a smile.

It was almost dark by the time the transfer of men and weapons had been completed.

Even before they reached the large dhow Bolitho could smell the stench of slavery. Once on board it was almost overpowering as the seamen and marines clambered below, stooping beneath the crude deck beams and slithering on filth and broken manacles.

Major Dewar's corporals were spaced at intervals along the hull to lead or push the new arrivals into the proper places where they would remain until the actual moment of attack. It was as well Eden had been left behind, Bolitho thought. This stench, and the cramped journey, would have made him as sick as a dog.

Several swivel guns were swayed up from the longboats and mounted on the bulwarks and aft by the high poop.

There was a smell of rum in the air too, and Bolitho guessed that the captain had thought it prudent to give the attackers something to sustain them.

Bolitho and the other two midshipmen made their way aft to the poop to report that all the extra seamen and marines were crammed below like pork in a barrel.

In the half-darkness the marines' cross-belts stood out very white, their coats merging with the background.

Hoggett, the *Gorgon*'s leather-lunged boatswain, was in charge of the dhow's sails and steering, and Bolitho heard one seaman mutter unkindly, ' 'E'd be right at 'ome on a blessed slaver, 'e would!'

Verling snapped, 'Break out the anchor and get this vessel under way, Mr Hoggett! Perhaps the wind will take the stench out of her!'

He turned as another shadowy figure climbed to the poop.

'All ready, Mr Tregorren?'

Dancer said, 'So he's coming too, damn him!'

'Anchor's aweigh, sir!'

Bolitho watched the two seamen using the great sweep oar which stood in place of wheel or tiller. The strange lateen sails creaked up the masts, the sailors slipping and cursing with unfamiliar, and to them, crude rigging.

Verling had brought a small boat's compass, and handed it to the boatswain.

'We will take our time. Stand well offshore. I'd rather not finish the attack like that frigate ended her life, eh, Mr Tregorren? It must have been quite a moment.'

Tregorren sounded as if his breathing was hurting him.

He replied thickly, 'It was, sir.'

Verling dropped the matter.

'Mr Pearce, show the lantern to *Gorgon*.'

Bolitho saw the light blink briefly as Pearce lifted the shutter. Captain Conway would know they had started. In the small glow from the compass Bolitho saw Verling's beaky profile, and was suddenly glad he was in command.

He wondered what Tregorren would say to him when next they spoke. If he would continue his deception, or admit that he was not responsible for *Pegaso*'s destruction.

Verling's voice bit into his thoughts.

'If you have nothing to do, I suggest you sleep

until you are called. Otherwise I will discover a task of some enormity for you, even in this vessel!'

Hidden by the deepening darkness, Bolitho grinned broadly.

'Aye, aye, sir. Thank you, sir.'

He settled down against an ancient bronze cannon and rested his chin on his knees. Dancer joined him, and together they stared up at the tiny, pale stars, against which the dhow's great sails showed like wings.

'Here we go again, Martyn.'

Dancer sighed. 'But we kept together. That's the main thing.'

10

A Name to Remember

'WIND's backed again, sir!'

The boatswain's hoarse voice made Bolitho nudge Dancer with his elbow and rouse him.

He saw Verling and Tregorren consulting the compass, and when he looked up at the ragged main-mast pendant he saw it was lifting and whipping to a new thrust of wind. The sky was paler, and as he struggled to his feet he felt every muscle throbbing with cramp.

Verling commented flatly, 'We will beat clear of the headland nevertheless.' His arm shot out, black against the sky. 'There! I can see surf below the point!' The arm darted round. 'You midshipmen, get below and rouse the people. My compliments to Major Dewar, and tell him we will pass very close inshore. I want no marine or seaman on deck who has not been so ordered.'

A block squeaked, and Bolitho saw a large flag jerking up to the foremost lateen sail. In daylight it would be seen as a black one, similar to that worn by the *Pegaso*. He shivered, despite his excitement.

'Come on, Martyn, we'd better hurry.'

He retched and covered his mouth with his sleeve as he plunged down into the fat-bellied hold. In the glitter of a solitary lantern the crowded seamen and marines could have been another slave cargo. The realization came like an ice-cold shock. If this attack failed, the survivors would end as no better than the poor wretches released by Captain Conway. Although the corsair, Raïs Haddam, recruited many white mercenaries to man his ships and expand his grip across the trade routes, he had little love or respect for them. If half of what was said of him was true, it was more than likely he would keep captured British seamen to replace those very same slaves.

Dewar listened to his message and grunted.

' 'Bout time. I'm aching like a sick cow.'

Dancer coughed and gasped, 'I am glad *we* were on deck, sir.'

The marines exchanged glances and Dewar said, 'Spoiled young devils! It is the discomfort I object to. The smell is no worse than any field of battle.' He grinned at Dancer's nausea. 'Especially after a few days, when the crows have been at work, eh?'

He stood up, ducking under the beams. 'Marines, stand-to! Sar'nt Halse, inspect the weapons!'

Bolitho returned to the poop, and found to his surprise that it was already bright enough to see the land drifting abeam, the dancing spray amongst some angry-looking rocks.

Dancer murmured, 'A lee shore. If the first

lieutenant had taken an hour longer we'd have been hard put to beat clear.'

'Sir! I can see someone on the point!'

Verling raised a telescope. 'Yes. He's gone from view now. Probably a lookout of some kind. He won't get across to the island, but the cosair may have a sort of signalling arrangement.' He was thinking aloud.

The wind made the great sails bang noisily, and the poorly-made rigging looked as if it might tear apart at any second. But it must be stronger than it appeared, Bolitho decided. He watched Hoggett supervising the helmsmen, the easy way the dhow turned to starboard to let the nearest rocks slip past the quarter with a bare twenty feet to spare. The dhow handled well. He smiled tightly. So it should. Arab sailors were using them long before ships like *Gorgon* were even dreamed of.

Pearce said, 'There's the fortress.' He grimaced. 'God, it looks a mite larger from this side!'

It was still shrouded in gloom, with only the upper tower and battery catching the first feeble light.

There was a sharp bang, and for an instant Bolitho imagined the fortress had seen through Captain Conway's ruse and could not restrain the gunners from firing.

He ducked as a ball whipped high overhead and threw a fanlike waterspout amongst the rocks.

'*Sandpiper*, sir!' A seaman almost prodded Verling in his excitement to point across the larboard beam. '*She* fired!'

Verling lowered his glass and studied him coldly.

'Thank you. I did not imagine it was an act of God!'

Another shot banged out, and this time the ball smashed down across the bows in direct line with their approach.

Verling gave a thin smile. 'Let her fall off, Mr Hoggett. I *know* Mr Dallas has an excellent gun captain with him in *Sandpiper*, but we'll not take too many chances.'

The dhow tilted steeply as the helmsmen brought her further round towards the island.

'Fire the er, stern-chaser.'

Verling stood aside as some seamen who had been working on one of the old bronze cannons plunged a slow-match into the pitted touch-hole and jumped clear.

The ancient bronze barrel was almost worn out, but the resonant bang was far louder than anyone had expected.

Verling said, 'That should do it. If we fire it again, I fear it will explode in our midst.'

Bolitho saw the brig for the first time. Close-hauled on a converging tack, she was heeling well over to the wind, her sails merged into one pale pyramid in the dawn light.

He saw the flash of another gun, and winced as the ball pounded close to the waterline, dousing seamen and crouching marines in falling spray.

Verling remarked angrily, 'Mr Dallas is too good an actor. A few more like that and I will have to take him to task.' He smiled at the boatswain. '*Later*, of course.'

'He's worried.' Dancer peered through the bulwark. 'I've never heard him make jokes before.'

'*Listen!*' Verling held up his hand. 'A trumpet! We've roused them at last!'

He became serious. 'Divide up the people, Mr Tregorren. You know what to do. There is some kind of jetty on the eastern side, right beneath the fortress. I am told it is where the traders bring the slaves, and from whence they ferry them to seagoing vessels.'

He placed his hat on the deck and glanced quickly at the others around him.

'Remove any items of uniform which might be recognized, and keep out of sight as much as possible. Pass the word to the marines to stand fast and wait for the order. *No matter what.*'

The brig was closing fast, several of her snappy six-pounders loosing-off shot, some of which fell dangerously near to the dhow.

A great boom shattered the air, and seconds later Bolitho saw a waterspout shoot skywards just beyond *Sandpiper*'s bowsprit.

Her sails were in disarray as Lieutenant Dallas brought her even closer, running up his ensign to the gaff as if to further infuriate the enemy.

Several more flashes lit the battery wall, and the splashes, although as big as the first, were haphazard and nowhere near the brig.

Bolitho supposed that the gun crews were still half-asleep, or could not believe that a vessel so frail, one which had already been seized below these same cannon, would dare press any nearer.

He bit his lip as another heavy ball passed between the brig's two masts. It was a miracle that neither was hit, but he saw several lengths of cut rigging drifting in the wind like jungle creeper.

One direct hit in a vital spot was all the battery needed to render the *Sandpiper* helpless. At least long enough for her to drive ashore and be taken.

Verling's voice was right in his ear.

'Don't keep staring at *Sandpiper*. Keep your eyes and mind ahead. We could be quite wrong about the entrance. Mr Starkie's memory may have played tricks on him.'

Bolitho darted a quick glance at Verling. Without his hat to balance it, the nose looked even beakier and larger. He saw something else on his face. Determination, anxiety, both were there. But also a kind of recklessness.

Bolitho looked away. He had seen a similar expression on the face of a highwayman as he had been driven to the gibbet.

Sunlight felt its way gingerly over the land and played across the fortress walls. There were several heads peering from the weathered embrasures, and then Bolitho saw what appeared to be a flagstaff poking out of the ground at the foot of the furthest wall.

Verling had already seen it.

'The entrance.' He turned to Hoggett. 'That must be a mast, just inside. Another dhow most likely.' He wiped his narrow face with the back of his arm. 'Steer for it.'

Tregorren hurried aft, hard put to hide his great

bulk beneath the litter of spare sails and fishing gear which covered the slaver's filthy deck from side to side.

'All ready, sir.'

He saw Bolitho and met his gaze without blinking. Defiance? It was difficult to see any emotion in the man. Even his colour was returning, and Bolitho wondered what would happen if he found time to take more drink before the attack.

'*Sandpiper*'s going about, sir. She's going to try another attack.'

Bolitho held his breath as two balls fell on either side of the brig's sleek hull, as with sails flapping and banging she turned across the wind's eye for another attempt to head off the dhow.

He saw the first sunlight shining on weapons above the battery wall and imagined the defenders jeering at the brig's retreat. Small she might be, and recaptured from them was a hard fact to swallow. But she was still a symbol of power of the world's greatest navy. And now, against their massive cannon, she was as helpless as a sick horse.

'There are men on the jetty, sir!' Pearce was in the bows, kneeling beside one of the swivels. 'They're watching us.'

Bolitho saw Hoggett's weatherbeaten face harden. The next minutes were vital. If the pirates suspected what was happening, the guns would soon be firing down on them. At this range there was no escape. And in a few more moments the island would lie between them and safety.

He felt his stomach rumbling noisily and glanced quickly at Dancer. His friend was breathing very quickly, and jumped as Bolitho gripped his shoulder and pulled him down to the deck.

Bolitho tried to smile. 'If they see your fair hair, they'll know we are not likely to be friendly!'

He turned as Verling snapped, 'Well said. I should have thought of that myself.' He turned away, already thinking far ahead of the slow-moving dhow.

The guns were firing again, but the sound was muffled, for the brig was hidden now by the fortress.

Nearer, and nearer. Bolitho tried to lick his lips as the top of the main fortress showed itself above the bulwark where he lay. Did the enemy recognize the dhow? Had she been here before?

He glanced up at Verling, who was standing with his arms folded beside the helmsmen. One of the latter was a Negro, of whom there were several in *Gorgon*'s company. It would make the little group seem genuine, he thought, and Verling certainly looked every inch a slaver.

'Take in the mains'l.'

Sunlight flooded into the deck as the mass of patched canvas and leather lashings came tumbling into the hull.

There were a dozen or more figures at the end of the jetty. Motionless, with only their long white robes lifting to the wind as the dhow edged round the crumbling stonework. Beyond the jetty there was a high, cavelike entrance, directly below the main wall. Several small vessels were moored there, and the largest one, a dhow, very like their prize, was tied up at the outer end, unable to dip her masts beneath the curved archway.

Thirty feet. Twenty.

Then a man yelled something and a figure ran to the steps to peer down at the dhow with sudden alarm.

Verling called tightly, 'Put her alongside! They're on to us!'

Then he tore his sword from its scabbard and was leaping long-legged from the poop before Hoggett's men had begun to lever their great oar.

Everything seemed to happen at once. From the bows and the bulwark the swivel guns were bared and fired at extreme angle into the men on the jetty. Those in the front fell kicking and screaming before a torrent of canister shot, and others caught on the end of the wall were cut down by the swivel on the poop.

Bolitho found his legs were taking him after the lieutenant, although he did not remember moving from the bulwark. Seamen surged from the hatches, cheering and yelling as they hurled themselves over the side and began to run for the entrance. Muskets banged from the wall and a few seamen fell before they had gone twenty yards.

But shock and surprise were taking effect. Perhaps the defenders had grown complacent and careless. Too long treated to the spectacle of terrified, beaten slaves being driven up this same jetty. The charging mob of seamen, the lethal glitter of cutlass blades and axes held some of them spellbound, so that when the *Gorgon*'s men swept amongst them they were cut down where they stood.

'Follow me, *Gorgons*!' Verling's voice needed no trumpet. '*At 'em!*'

As they ran haphazardly beneath the archway and past some smaller boats there was a rattle of musket fire from the fortress itself, as at long last the defenders were made to realize what was happening.

Gasping and cursing, their legs apart, chests heaving painfully, the attacking sailors were slowly compressed by two adjoining walls, their advance steadily reduced as more and more men came from the wall above.

Bolitho locked swords with a great giant, who mouthed and screamed with every savage slash of his heavy blade. He felt something slide against his ribs and heard the seaman, Fairweather, gasp, 'Take *that* then!'

The touch had been Fairweather's pike, which was almost dragged from his grasp as the pirate toppled shrieking over the side of the stairs.

But other seamen were falling. Bolitho could feel his shoes catching on sprawled limbs as he lurched shoulder to shoulder with Dancer and Hoggett, their arms aching, their swords and hangers as heavy as lead.

Someone pitched sideways and was trampled underfoot.

Bolitho only got one glance. It was Midshipman Pearce, his eyes already dull and without recognition as blood ran from his mouth.

Sobbing, half blind with sweat, Bolitho drove his sword-hilt against a man's head who was trying to strike at a wounded seaman. As he lurched away he turned his blade, felt his balance steady on one foot and then drove it under the pirate's armpit.

Verling was yelling, '*Stand fast, lads!*' There was blood on his neck and chest, and he was almost separated from the bulk of his men by slashing, screaming pirates.

Bolitho turned as Dancer let out a cry and dropped amongst the others. He had slipped on some blood, and as he fell his hanger clattered away out of reach.

He rolled over, staring wide-eyed as a robed figure ran at him with a raised scimitar.

Bolitho tried to cut a man down to reach him, but was in turn knocked aside as Tregorren charged through the mob like a bull and slashed the pirate across the face, opening it from ear to chin.

Then above the cries and clash of steel Bolitho heard the blare of a trumpet, followed instantly by Major Dewar's thick, familiar tones.

'*Marines! Advance!*'

Bolitho dragged his friend away from the interlocked figures, holding him clear of thrusting blades, his mind cringing from noise and hate.

Verling's reckless attack had been for one thing only. To lure down the bulk of the pirates from the wall to defend the entrance from the dhow's crew. What it must have been like for the marines, crouching in the hold, hearing their messmates and friends being butchered while they waited for the signal to advance, Bolitho could barely imagine.

But they were coming now. Their scarlet coats and white cross-belts shone in the sunlight as if on parade, and as Verling waved his sword to call his seamen back from the stairs, Major Dewar bellowed, '*Front rank, fire!*'

The musket balls swept through the packed bodies on the stairs, and as the marines paused to reload, their ramrods rising and falling as one, the next rank marched through them, knelt, took aim and fired.

It was more than enough, the defenders broke and stampeded through the entrance.

Dewar lifted his sword. 'Fix bayonets! Marines, *charge*!'

Yelling like madmen, his men forgot their discipline and lunged for the entrance.

'*Huzza! Huzza!*' The seamen, breathless and bleeding, lowered their weapons as the marines charged past.

Dancer said, 'Let's get George out of the way.'

Together they dragged Pearce's spread-eagled body into the shadow of the wall. He was staring straight up at the sky, the shock of death frozen on his face.

Hoggett was shouting, 'Through 'ere, sir!' He gestured at some great iron-studded doors. 'It's full of slaves!'

Bolitho stood up shakily and took a firmer grip on his curved hanger. He caught Tregorren's eye, and the lieutenant asked curtly, 'You all right?'

He replied shakily, 'Aye, sir.'

Tregorren nodded. 'Right. Take some hands and follow the marines –' He paused as a sound like distant thunder rolled across the bay and against the headland. Then came the crash of iron, the clatter of falling stonework.

Verling wrapped a rag around one bloodied wrist and tightened the knot with his teeth.

'*Gorgon* has arrived.' It was all he said.

Again and again, the seventy-four poured a broad-side into the island fortress. The bombardment made little difference to the defences, but attacked and harried from within by the jubilant marines, and with two ships-of-war sailing unhampered below the wall, it was enough.

Major Dewar appeared at the top of the steps, his hat gone, a deep cut above one eye. But he was able to grin as he reported that the defence had crumbled.

To prove his words, the black flag above the battery floated down like a dying bird, and was replaced, to wild cheering, by one of the ship's ensigns.

Their minds still shocked by the savage fighting, they climbed the steps to the high ramparts where the unmanned guns pointed impotently across the blue water. There were dead and dying everywhere, and too many red coats sprawled amongst the rest.

Bolitho and Dancer stood on the wall and watched the ships far below. The little brig was already quivering in the early haze, but *Gorgon* was clear-cut and splendid as she tacked ponderously towards the island, her depleted topmen shortening sail, but pausing to wave and shout towards the figures on the wall, their cheers lost in distance.

It was very quiet, and when Bolitho looked at Dancer he saw there were tears cutting through the grime on his cheeks.

Bolitho said, 'Easy, Martyn.'

'I was thinking of George Pearce. How it was nearly me. And you.'

Bolitho turned to watch as *Gorgon*'s great anchor plummeted into the placid water.

He said quietly, 'I know. But we are alive, and must be grateful.'

Verling's shadow merged with theirs.

'God blast your eyes!' He glared at the pair of them. 'Do you think I can do everything on my own?' He looked past them at the ship and gave a tired smile. 'But I know how you feel.' The strain dropped from his sharp features like a shadow. 'I never thought I'd live to see that old lady again!' He swung away, already barking orders.

Bolitho watched him gravely. 'Well, it shows you never really know a man.'

They pushed themselves from the wall, as wearily, obediently, the seamen and marines began to muster beneath the flag.

When Verling spoke again to the assembled men his tone was as usual.

'Smarten yourselves up. Remember this, and remember it well. You are *Gorgons*. It is a reputation hard to live by.' For the briefest instant his glance fell on Bolitho. 'Often easy to die for. Now, clap the prisoners in irons and attend to our wounded. After that' – he looked up and beyond the gently-flapping flag, as if surprised to be able to see either – 'we will take care of those who were less fortunate.'

By evening most of the wounded had been ferried across to the anchored *Gorgon*. The dead were buried on the island beneath the wall, where Bolitho heard

an old seaman say as he leaned on his spade, 'I
reckon this place'll be fought over again an' again.
These poor lads will get the best view of it next time.'

As shadow hid the scars of *Gorgon*'s bombardment,
Dancer and Bolitho stood side by side on the larboard gangway watching the last rays holding on to
the drooping flag above the battery.

Despite a careful search, they had found no trace
of Raïs Haddam. Perhaps he had escaped, or had
never been in the fortress at all. The pirates would
say nothing about him, or betray his whereabouts.
They were more frightened of Haddam than they
were of their captors. The latter offered only death
by hanging.

It would all have to be sorted out by Captain
Conway, Bolitho thought wearily, his eyelids drooping. The slaves to be ferried ashore, the battery
spiked and thrown into the sea. So many things.

A step fell on the deck behind them and they
turned, lurching upright as the captain paused to
speak. He was impeccably dressed. The same as if
nothing had happened, and none had died.

He examined them impassively. 'The first lieutenant informs me that you all did very well. I am
glad to know it.' His gaze shifted slightly. 'Mr Bolitho,
he told me that you in particular acted with the
finest qualities of a King's officer. I shall mention as
much in my report to the admiral.'

He nodded curtly and strode aft towards the poop.

Dancer turned, his smile fading as he saw Bolitho
bent over the nettings, his shoulders shaking un-
controllably.

But Bolitho faced him again, gripping his friend's arm to reassure him.

Between gasps he managed to explain. 'Things *have* changed, Martyn. *The captain remembered my name!*'